To the people of the world.

David Ssembajjo

Mr Batwala's Farm

Austin Macauley Publishers™
London • Cambridge • New York • Sharjah

A CIP catalogue record for this title is available from the British Library.

ISBN 9781528929431 (Paperback)
ISBN 9781528929448 (Hardback)
ISBN 9781528965873 (ePub e-book)

www.austinmacauley.com

First Published (2019)
Austin Macauley Publishers Ltd
25 Canada Square
Canary Wharf
London
E14 5LQ

Chapter One
Mr Batwala's Farm

Mr Batwala was a well-known drunkard in his village. He was fond of stroking his goatee and he was seated in his office listening to coffee prices on the *BBC World Service*. He wanted to find out the level of prices; if they were good, he would continue to open the farm and if they were bad or low, he would need to find drastic ways to continue running the farm but that would be unacceptable to his workers. He would continue trading employing many people in the village. It was believed that Mr Batwala got his wealth from his family. Mr Batwala's office was old and it was rough. Mr Batwala was fond of throwing rubbish in various unimaginable places in the office where rats and cockroaches were summoned to feast on food scraps. In his office, he had pictures of the great and the good. His farm was a pilot farm and people across the land came to inspect the goodness of the farm. The government rewarded Mr Batwala with privileges and showered him with gifts. Mr Batwala employed his workers to work all year round including weekends without respite or rest. On this sunny day, Mr Batwala went out to work where he was held on his two feet by his workers as they thought he was unstable due to heavy drinking which Mr Batwala was fond of and he later returned to his office. There came a priest on Sunday to try and preach the Good News to the workers and also to campaign for the reservation of Sunday as a day of rest as requested by God to keep the Sabbath as a day of rest (as he rested on the seventh day). The priest Father Motala came out of the friary alone. He wanted to make men and women fear God. The priest made sermons by trying to bar and intercept workers who were laden with coffee baskets strapped at their backs. He pleaded with them and began preaching as they passed him giving him deaf ears.

'Stop all your work and listen to the work of God. God made the world in six days and rested on the seventh and you should all rest on the Sabbath… please keep this day for rest.'

'We are busy, stop your sermons; go to your church, lock yourself there and keep to your priestly life… take care of yourself in church and forget about us, we are in no need of sermons that cannot provide a meal for the day. Please we would ask you to leave,' said one worker.

Father Motala insisted on preaching whereby he took out a Bible and began reading Genesis and how God made the world – man and woman into his image. He read out the Lord's Prayer. As soon as he was praying to the workers who passed him, some became interested in what he had to say due to curiosity, some peered at the priest and a small crowd of workers formed and stood detached around the priest giving up their work and duties in order to listen to the priest.

'You must all come to church and to rest on the Sabbath. God took a rest on the seventh day and gave the world this Sabbath to respect all that God made for God will punish you for the desecration of this Sabbath,' Father Motala said, waving the bible in mid-air.

'Get back to work, we are working for life on earth if you want to let God help in your church,' the head of workers commanded.

'The Jews were well off in Egypt and your workers cannot be saved from all your toiling authority to make them labour worse than oxen. God does not live on money, please give up all your work on the Sabbath.'

'I have a house to build and I chose to work on the farm for it to enable me to complete it as it is the only source which can assist me to see through my house. I am dependent on the farm for all my living; without the farm I would be nowhere yet all my possessions come from the farm,' Mulata the head of the workers said.

'All the money we have comes from the farm and the whole village relies on the farm; if the farm fails, we all fail as a result.'

'But God needs no money to look after the world… who has ever paid God for all the work he has done for the earth. Praise the Lord Alleluia. He will come back to save the world, you will suffer damnation.'

Most people had ceased work and they were debating the situation. The priest Father Motala was the only priest to come out of the friary leaving his fellow priests behind and he never consulted any of them and he falsified his whereabouts and never reported on any of his absences, yet many of the priests thought he had settled into church business and he told his fellow priests that he would be having a walk and all his moves were not monitored. He took liberties and never compromised about his whereabouts and what he had done out of the friary. Yet the rest of the priests never ventured out, they were always praying and working over church duties, having priestly meetings and locking themselves away in prayer and sermons. They met to discuss their lives and livelihood. Father Motala did not account for his walks and there were no entry books to sign for any journeys incurred by him. Father Motala was dressed in cassock and walked along with a staff. The farm workers were singing and their songs were heard easily in Mr Batwala's office. The workers were pruning and weeding and also picking coffee and later drying them in the sun to harden in real coffee instants, yet others were loading the coffee beans on trucks. Mr Batwala's office building seemed as if it would collapse as it was built in a rush. The walls were dangling only held up by pillars of wood and when the gust of wind arrived, they creaked and shook sideways. Mr Batwala heard the sermons from the priest and he had bitter confrontations with the priest on a number of occasions. Mr Batwala sent away and banned Father Motala from giving his sermons to his workers and they never agreed on any issue. Mr Batwala heard the sound and voice of the priest saying 'Praise the Lord Alleluia' which was coming from the middle of the farm. Mr Batwala walked out of his office and went to face and attend to the priest who was disrupting the farm. Mr Batwala approached the priest.

'What are you trying to achieve on this farm which you want to disrupt,' said Mr Batwala.

'You should rest on a Sunday and preserve this day for the Lord God.'

'I cannot listen to any of your words.'

'Listen and believe.'

'I cannot accept your sermons. Could you all workers return back to work and leave Father Motala and never listen to him.

He wants to ruin the farm.' Mulata was told to herd the workers back to work and he went telling each one to return back to work.

'Listen, don't leave as I have good news to tell you. Stop there please and be faithful to your lives.'

The workers dispersed even though Father Motala tried to hinder them. They all returned to work even though they wished to listen to the sermons of Father Motala. They were all caught up in a vicious circle of being able to stay and listen to the priest and juggle together work on hand and no worker was left to listen to the sermons of the priest. Father Motala and Mr Batwala were left on their own to iron out their differences. Mr Batwala on several occasions had sent away the priest for disrupting the farm and he chased him away. But the priest kept on with his sermons and insisted on his continuation to convert. Mr Batwala walked back to his office followed behind by the priest who tracked each step that Mr Batwala took. Father Motala preached but Mr Batwala was not interested and detested each word that the priest mentioned.

'Follow the way of God and you need God to bring rain to water your farm. Do you pay God for all that work?'

'I am looking after people and they gain from the farm and all things they require come from the farm. God looks after the world that is God's duty and man looks after all men, women, and children. God looks after me, you, and all my workers that is the generosity. We are supposed to look after the world that God gave us, look after it well as long as there is God. That is the responsibility or rioting in any way and there is peace. People are willing to work and have no cause to cause warfare.'

Father Motala was listening to what Mr Batwala said and he was not impressed with what he heard. The two men entered Mr Batwala's office and inside were bottles of Ugandan Waragi which Mr Batwala drank. The bottles were thrown about in a rush and disorder. Inside them were cobwebs, cockroaches. Pieces of paper were laid out on top of the table and no one could make out what each letter contained. There were rubbish and leftovers which found their place in all sorts of places, there were strewn bones and the office gave a stale smell of staleness.

'It is the responsibility of man to create peace and God blesses that peace. I created this farm in three hundred and sixty-five days a year and there was no rebellion or no one fought, yet people were idle and I employed them and the village has developed as a result of this farm. The farm came out of peace and not war. Yet the peace of the farm has extended beyond the farm,' Mr Batwala rumbled in excitement.

Mr Batwala sat down across his executive table. He took a ledger book and began calculating sums as he was responsible for balances in the books and making figures, in the background the sound of singing workers could easily be heard. Mr Batwala scribbled on another piece of paper which he took out of a drawer. He took out again from the drawer a balance sheet and came up with good figures which meant that the farm was performing well.

'Why don't you give alms and save the world. Be like the poor widows who gave all she had to the Church yet those who have plenty have not given as much from their lot. Why gain the world to forsake God and the Kingdom of Heaven.'

'The Church is looking for alms but I have already given to the Church by helping to set up the farm and I have helped mankind already. We are all looking for money and God looks after us. Why doesn't the Church give alms to save the world; it must equal for both laity and priests to give alms to save the world.'

'The Church cannot,' Father Motala said and made a sign of the cross.

'The Church is a great beggar and scrounger. Why does it hide its source of income and pay little leap-service to all men. Can't the Church look after itself as we are all maintaining our lives?'

'The Church must have followers to survive and it cannot rely on itself. We in the church are beggars and relying on the general public for the greater good.'

'So you came here looking for followers to rely on. How much can a man give in order to enter the kingdom of God?'

'You should give this day for resting and make it holy.'

'We rest each passing day when we come off work, when we have the day off.'

Mr Batwala wished to drink his spirit of Ugandan Waragi and felt as if he should give Father Motala some yet Mr Batwala knew point blank that the priest had never tasted any spirit. Father Motala wanted to gain wealth for himself and not for the other priests in the friary and he knew he would succeed if he interacted with the general public and would stakeout his unopposed position which would lead him to wealth. The only way that Mr Batwala could expel Father Motala was to give him the strong drink.

'I have a present to give you.'

'What have you to offer me?'

'It is my golden calf and it tastes well and strong.'

Mr Batwala had wrapped the drink in calico cloth and he caressed his bottle with eagerness and with great interest. He sipped his drink and handed the bottle to the priest. Father Motala looked at the bottle and he was puzzled and dismayed but was impressed about the whole spectacle but felt like he should have the drink in secrecy not to give an example to the general public who, if they found out, would make a mockery of the priesthood and the Church and the Church would not have followers. Father Motala wished to take the drink in total isolation and away from the public glare. He stood in uneasy silence looking at Mr Batwala sipping his drink and practically did not resist his hand from trying to raise the bottle over his mouth but instead rose the bottle over his nose to smell the drink. However, the weather was sunny and not too humid.

'Here have this drink and you shall have health, energy and power.'

'What sort of drink is it?'

'It is my golden calf better than your church. Have some to your health,' Mr Batwala said in a loud voice which echoed beyond the office into the entire village which woke the sleeping birds in nests, waking cattle in the kraal and sailing beyond the open seas which disturbed the whales and the voice of Mr Batwala made antelopes skip and caught short the hunting lions. Mr Batwala's voice attracted the workers who ceased their work.

Mr Batwala's voice made grazing sheep stop eating and looked beyond the ridges. Mr Batwala sipped and offered some to Father Motala who stood in patience and in expectant mood of some kind. The priest held the bottle observing it in great delight and eager anticipation at the prospect of drinking it. Father Motala was fearful and walked out of the office so to search if anybody observed him and to search that there were no priests in the vicinity, for he loved his job yet he went on prowling in the village, taking in all places. He searched the village as if he had lost precious metal. He prowled around the lake and he secretively inquired of the priests yet he left Mr Batwala in the office who thought that the priest had vanished. Father Motala reappeared that his investigation had brought no suspicions. None of the priests was present.

'Don't tell the whole world about me taking this drink. Not even your workers because they would inform the world that there is a drunk priest. I don't like this to reach the priests.'

Father Motala sipped Uganda Waragi and he became a little drunk and his vision was impaired and he thanked Mr Batwala and told him that he would hide it so that he could always have something to drink and he would hide it in the bird's nest and he would make the bird to look after it so that no one would steal from him and that he would pay the bird for its honest service for being the priests' banker. He would give the bird interest. Father Motala occasionally went to check on the bird's nest and climbed up the tree to taste the spirit which he was deeply endeared to and when asked why he had been climbing the tree he said it was to find honeycombs. Father Motala would sneak into the friary. The friary was nestled on a hilltop which was visible from all angles and was the most dominant feature on the hill and all activities in the area were shaped along the Church. Many priests were seen wandering about the friary in a long file praying as they walked and receiving blessings from Father Motala. Some prayers were heard by passers-by and no one could make up what the priests were praying and the priests listened to Father Motala about the daily routine. Duties and responsibilities were apportioned and delegated to all priests those that would take over the laundry, cooking roles and working in the tropical orchard or farm of tropical fruit and others were given cleaning and washing up or tidying up. Some other priests were sent on errands far from the friary. Some were told to lawn the friary grounds. Some ran the friary shop which sold bibles and other religious material and literature, which could gain them a superb reputation of being well versed in knowledge. Meanwhile, father Motala was preparing to return to the Church friary incognito and avoided been seen in public and Father Motala exploited the lax situation in the friary whereby each had his own place of rest out of reach from the other priests. Father Motala left Mr

Batwala's office and said that he should return to the farm to preach again about how God and Jesus would save the world from evil and wickedness and wanton exploitation by Mr Batwala. The priest said he would teach the workers on the virtues of the Lord God. So Father Motala left the office with his drink and went on to sing and pray.

Meanwhile on the farm, Mzeei, one of the workers, was picking coffee when he was accidentally bitten by a snake and he became rather uneasy and other workers surrounded to heal him, and he was offered first aid to regain his mood and stability, and the workers decided to lift him up. News reached his family as he was the breadwinner for a complete hundred members of his extended family who all relied on Mzeei. They all came weeping and fearing for the worst. Mzeei was carried to the office. All work had ceased and felt they should know the fate of Mzeei. Mr Batwala had run out of his spirit and was on the verge of leaving his office to buy a drink for himself but was surprised to see that all workers had left the jobs unattended to and Mzeei lay at the entrance of the door and a small crowd had formed which included all workers, Mzeei's family and the whole village of Bukuku.

'Mr Batwala, we have heard with sadness the news of our father Mzeei being unstable because he was bitten by a snake. We feel that you should compensate him for his injuries as we all depend on him and he is the breadwinner in our family,' Jayal said. She was the wife of Mzeei.

'I cannot give you any money as I am not an insurance company and I am not a bank. I am not a hospital to look after sick people and if they can't work I cannot pay them all I need them is for them to be able-bodied individuals.'

'Who shall feed us in this world?'

'Not even a priest can help you come out of the whole world to help Mzeei earn a living yet God looks after the world.'

'Who shall look after us if Mzeei is gone and is unable to work? We all rely on Mzeei and he is no more. Where on earth we will suffer,' Jayal said.

'I cannot pay any money to you or any member of your family. I want a drink and I have to leave to buy one. I cannot presently attend to your needs. Do you understand? I am thirsty for a drink and I need to leave. Take away your man.'

‘Where can we take him? Let us take him to church; maybe they would look after him and pray for him and he would soon recover and we shall celebrate to his life,’ Jayal said.

‘I will lock you out of my office.’

The entourage of Mzeei took him to the Church and all workers followed the family to the Church where they met Father Motala. They gave him details of what had happened and told him Mr Batwala had refused to give them any money as sick pay. Father Motala stressed he would require money to pray for Mzeei. Father Motala insisted that his prayer would make Mzeei recover. The workers had money but none would lend it to the family. It was left for the family to find other means to raise the required money. The family promised Father Motala that they would pay him once they have received their wages. Father Motala instructed that Mzeei should be taken to his bed for him to offer prayers. Mzeei was laid to sleep on his bed where the priest poured holy water and made a sign of the cross on Mzeei’s forehead. He sprinkled the holy water on the snakebite and he gave out the praying saying:

‘In the Lord we have a saviour, he gives life and takes it away. In the Lord lies forgiveness. He loves those that search for him. He guides and protects them from all scourges. He disciplines and his love endures forever. The Lord takes pity on all his servants he keeps away from trouble, he gives your heart’s desire and you don’t suffer from want. He will not withdraw his hand from helping you. Ask for help and the Lord will not fail to provide. He tries one more than how steel is forged. The Lord blesses life and you shall delight in your life in the light of God you shall shine all to see because God is your refuge. Amen.’

‘Amen.’

Father Motala pleaded with the family and workers whereby he said that all of them worked and encouraged people to work on Sundays and only remembered God when they were in trouble. In the meantime, Father Motala went back to his church friary.

Mr Batwala had finished his work on Sunday and felt it appropriate to take Father Motala to his paradise, as he called it. He decided to visit Father Motala in his church. Reaching the Church he noticed a herd boy watering his cattle and he asked for the boy to help have some water for his thirst. The borehole was a contested point of place with vicious acrimonious disputes and it was the only place where the whole village obtained its fresh drinking water. Many wars were staged around the water hole. The boy had insisted that his cattle should have a go first but relented and pumped the water for Mr Batwala to drink. In front of the Church grounds was an avocado tree with birds perched on top of it. There were priests in the grounds of the Church and when they saw Mr Batwala approaching them, they quickly walked into the Church friary and closed the door behind them. Mr Batwala called out to them but they never responded but walked away quietly.

'Father Motala,' Mr Batwala called out several times.

But no priest responded. The priests rarely came into contact with the general public but kept to themselves. Mr Batwala forced the door and it opened. He walked to the chancery and looked at the empty church. He called out for Father Motala.

'Father Motala, it is me Mr Batwala. I have come to take you to my paradise, come out.'

No one responded at all and no one was available to help on hand. Mr Batwala decided to leave and as he was walking out of the door, Father Motala appeared.

'Oh, Father Motala it is nice to see you. I came to invite you to my paradise where all workers meet to have a rest.'

'There is one paradise in the world and that is heaven.'

'You will like it and would not hate it at all.'

'Why did you call me? You my fellow priests detest visitors and none among them ever receives a visitor.'

'Why let yourself close in when you have the world around you.'

'Where is your paradise?'

'Don't worry.'

'I have to worry and all you mean is to take me out and make a fool of me,' Father Motala said.

Both men walked along a dirt road and continued to speak of paradise.

'It is a bar of paradise where you enjoy all things and to indulge in all kinds of things.'

'I wouldn't like that.'

'Come along and judge for yourself,' Mr Batwala stressed and argued on.

Both men reached the bar which was reeling with excitement, laughter, singing, clapping and dancing, music and the bar was located in the centre of the village.

'Welcome, Mr Batwala and Father Motala,' all workers in the bar beamed and shouted several times.

Some workers clapped their hands and danced and they were very euphoric on seeing the two men. They offered their seats to the two men. Mr Batwala ordered drinks, food and Father Motala declined to drink and eat. Five concubines of Mr Batwala came along to join Mr Batwala at the table. The concubines fed Mr Batwala on chicken drumsticks, feeding him as a mother feeds her young. All concubines wished to ask Mr Batwala for financial assistance.

'Jagala, what do you want from me, my dear?' Mr Batwala enquired.

'I want one million shillings to build my house.'

'There you are with one million.'

Mr Batwala signed a cheque and gave it to Jagala.

'I am Chama I want two hundred thousand shillings.'

'There you are with this cheque.'

'I am Hama and I want five million.'

'There you are with your lot.'

'I am Baluma, I want two million.'

'There you are with two million. What of my favourite Jamula?' Mr Batwala asked.

'I want ten million.'

'Here with ten million and use that cheque well.'

'Why don't you give all that money to the Church; it could make good use of it?' Father beamed out.

'Has the Church given me any money or come to my help?'

'I am totally disgusted with your waste. All your workers are wasteful, all of them are wasteful and none to the rescue.'

'Give Father Motala a drink and the drink will save the world,' Mr Batwala yelled out in great amazement.

'Drink to our health,' the workers said.

'I will not drink to your health,' Father Motala spoke out emphatically.

Mr Batwala called for a guitar to play some popular tunes. The waiters gave Mr Batwala a guitar which he played dexterously after caressing the guitar as a young child is cared for. He danced while he played the guitar. He wanted to encourage Father Motala to drink to his health and all men in the bar got to their feet to dance and cheer everybody who was around. Some men and women sang, cheering on, clapping hands they all formed a circle to dance and all underwent through a period of enchantment which made the dust rise over the bar into the higher skies above and it disappeared away by means of prolonged wind and breeze. The workers laughed to praise the priest but Father Motala was not impressed by gestures of kindness and mercies which followed the songs and dancing. The priest walked out of the bar which was reeling with extensive excitement, joy and with all joviality involved. Father Motala came back to the bar as he was being followed and pursued by the workers to encourage to get more involved with the excitement that prevailed. The priest asked for an accordion to play for the soul of the workers who had resisted his conversion. He was adamant about his ability to make people believe in his sermons.

Chapter Two

The workers after finishing work felt hungry and decided to go to church to beg for food. As word went around that the Church had some free meals offered to the poor of the village and they all wanted to queue for food which was not paid for. They all gathered at the Church entrance with empty bowls and waited on patiently to be directed on how to obtain the food. The workers called for Father Motala.

'What can I do for you?' Father Motala asked and bemoaned.

'We are hungry we were looking for food, Can you give us some food.'

'You must give me all your yearly wages before I can offer you food and if you don't have money, you can give all your life properties including all your belongings and if you have none, I will take all the clothes you are wearing or I will take all your jewellery and I will trade it and offer your belongings to the highest bidder.'

'We have nothing to offer apart for life.'

'Nothing is for free.'

'We have no money to offer but we promise we shall pay you later,' some workers pleaded.

'I cannot agree with that we are dealing with scarce resources for only a few who can afford.'

'We definitely shall pay you.'

'The Church needs money and it cannot be a servant and slave of the whole world.'

The workers grumbled about what the priest said and they were confused. They fell into arguments that resulted in fistfights which were not easily containable. They blamed the priest for the chaos and confusion, and they said they would lodge a case in court to accuse the priest.

‘We shall pay you, and we make a verbal agreement that under all circumstances you shall get paid,’ one worker said.

‘Okay, let me trust you. You can all go and search for food in the orchard.’

The Church orchard had all sorts of tropical fruits which included pineapples, passion fruits, mangoes, jackfruit, guavas and sugarcane. The workers rushed into the orchard and some tumbling down and there was a stampede as they all searched for fruit. They foraged and ate the fruit leaving behind a litter of fruit along the pathways. They rampaged and struggled in a stampede and were still left hungry. The orchard was emptied of all fruit as if there was no other day to feast. They asked Father Motala for more food and Father Motala ordered priests to prepare meals for the workers. After preparing the meals for the workers, they were invited to the crypt where the food had been prepared. The workers raised their bowls in mid-air and all food was cooked leaving the priests with nothing of their own to feed on. The priests did not have anything to eat; they went out to the centre of the village to sell their belongings, church memorabilia and barter their holy water and wine the blood of Christ which was reserved for church services.

‘Here is a church bell that summons the laity to church,’ the priests said. It was as if the priests were auctioning the kingdom of heaven, so that people may have part of it. They were as if they were selling everything that heaven had to provide as if heaven was there to be auctioned without the permission of God. Can heaven be valued?

‘I have a crucifix,’ one priest urged on.

‘Here with a cassock,’ another said.

‘Here with a staff,’ another repeated.

‘Here with the bible and all its times,’ said another priest.

People gathered to watch the priest’s trade. They all realised how vulnerable the world of priesthood had become. It was if they were selling heaven which no man could value but the priest alone could value it at no cost to their lives. Some people went ahead to inquire of the goods put on sale. The Church it seems would come to an end. However, the priests pressed on firmly and none succeeded and they all failed in their attempt to sell anything.

Pay Day

The workers on Mr Batwala's farm prepared themselves for payday. They had duties to attend, some had financial responsibilities to look out for. The workers had to depend and rely on the farm to provide all their needs and demands. Some had begun prematurely to set up business as an extra hand on resources or extra income. The village could only exist because of the existence of the farm. Some had debts to settle and others had calculated their income in order to afford commodities, clothes and some had wishes of buying cattle, goats, sheep and chickens. Mulata, the head or leader of the workers, was building a house and it was half finished and had not reached completion and he had a long way to go to finish it; he had to buy building material, cement, mortar, tiles, pipes and electrical goods, windows, doorframes, nails, flooring plaster, metal beams, ceiling grills and all roofing requirements. Mulata had measured and counted his wages and he knew he could afford it. He was happy and jovial that all his hard work would be paid off. God had granted him his wish to finish the house. Mulata led the workers in front to be paid by Mr Batwala. Mr Batwala took out the pay book which included the number of days each worker had worked and what post each held on the farm. The book had the total names of the workers and the time they had worked on the farm. This was not a good day because the prices of coffee were down than in the past. Mr Batwala sat down to pay the workers.

'Good morning, every day is not a sunny or rainy day… you cannot have rain for the whole year. I am the bearer of bad news for all of you. The prices of coffee are below the normal level. You will all have to settle for less pay than the usual pay. I have cut down your pay. You will receive less pay,' Mr Batwala announced.

'We cannot settle for less pay. I have a house to build yet it is half finished and this is the only work I know… where will I get money from to finish the house with this little pay,' Mulata complained and pleaded for answers.

'I want to buy food and clothes,' said one worker.

'I have to set up or buy premises for a shop but how will I be able to achieve that if I have little pay and I have the budget,' said one worker.

'I have a family to look after and how would I look after them if I receive little pay,' one female worker said.

'I am sick and I do not know where I will receive treatment without money…' another worker said.

'We shall not settle for less. I am Mulata; that is the fact.'

'We all agreed that payment must not change come Kingdom of God,' another female said.

'I have no influence on setting up the price of coffee, they set up the prices on world markets in London and America and a producer has no influence on those coffee prices. They care less about your wellbeing and welfare. If you can petition or lobby them to consider your needs, then go ahead otherwise you must accept this pay,' Mr Batwala elaborated.

'We shall not work until the right prices are restored,' Mulata moaned.

'You must work, even the bees' work, the ants work too and never get paid for the services rendered and I am dictating how much you should be paid. A goat cannot live on such little pay, those who dictate payments should come take up the work which we perform,' Mulata said.

'They should not dictate prices of coffee to determine our lives,' said one worker.

'It is better that we determine our prices because we are responsible for our work,' said Mulata. 'We are slaves to coffee. We are no masters.'

Mr Batwala paid the workers who lined up and all workers left and categorically refused to work for less pay. They deserted the farm in droves. They became idle and never took up work on the farm. Mr Batwala was left alone to work the land. He pruned, weeded, plucked coffee from the coffee trees, dried the coffee beans, collected coffee and loaded the trucks which plied the farm to deposit the coffee in coffee depots and factories. No single person came to his assistance and they laughed at Mr Batwala that he was carrying an elephant over his shoulders. People believed that he would collapse under the weight of his task that he had allocated himself. Yet, Mr Batwala was comfortable, he never gave up on his task and never abandoned his work on the farm. Mr Batwala was busy and overworked. Mr Batwala, while damping coffee husks on the farm, tripped and fell into the pit and was nearly being sucked into the pit but was lucky that Father Motala was on hand to deliver him from sinking into the pit of husks. Mr Batwala gave up work on the farm, as he had failed to convince people to return to work. He decided and opted to marry and he had children. Mr Batwala migrated to the city, moving into the city with his wife and two children.

Chapter Three

Mr Batwala had the largest brick house in Nakivubo slum in Kampala city. The house was in the centre of the slum. Well placed and no one failed to notice it for its precise position which dominated the skyline. Mr Batwala called for a party in the slum. The poorest of the poor came along and no guest was left out, there came the blind, lame, deaf and dumb. People played a variety of instruments such as drums, xylophones, flutes, cymbals, guitars, mouth organs yet some came with goods to sell to the guests at exorbitant prices. They haggled with guests and told them how poor they were and some came to beg as they found out it was a good opportunity to beg. Some set up shop to charge others for shoe shining and barbers cut hair at cut-price prices. People played tunes and the noise was deafening.

The poor began asking guests for cash. The blind wanted to campaign for leading the slum to clear the slum of litter and rubbish. They wanted to spruce up the slum. They wanted to organise the slum and requested people for a vote for them to carry out their duties as leaders. The able-bodied told the blind that it was impossible for them to vote for them as they did not have the power to elect them to lead the slum. Yet at the fringes of the slum traders set up shops, butchers sold meat to small roast meat sellers who sold the meat to guests, some sold food and illicit drinks which were banned and they sold this to customers clandestinely, and they first asked for identities of those that wanted or wished to buy the illicit drinks. People were dancing and celebrating the party. Mr Batwala summoned his guests to listen to his story of courage, a story that is compassionate to the blind or the disable. 'I have good tidings to bring to you. There was a leper and a rich man. There was a leper who begged and when the rich passed the leper who begged, the rich man brushed dust on the plate that the beggar had. The beggar one day was lonely, marooned on the streets when war broke out; he wanted shelter. So he looked for safety in the rich man's house but the rich man sent out hounds of dogs which bit the leper who suffered severely over his wounds. The dogs chased away the leper who ran away from them after being bitten. Then one day, there were floods and the leper swam to save the national vaults from being drown and swept away in the floods. The leper saved the nation's wealth. Then the president declared that all the disable should be rewarded and the president said that the leper should take away the rich man's wealth but he refused saying he needed nothing but required that all rich should be kind because they all rely on one another and everyone needs the help of one another that if all were treated badly no one benefits. Therefore beware of the disabled ladies and gentlemen,' Mr Batwala said.

Mr Batwala stood in the middle of his house and called on all his guests that had turned up for the party to take whatever they wanted or desired anything from his house.

'Ladies and gentlemen, you are welcome to take whatever you like from my house because I will live on fresh air which is costless and no man can put a price on it, it is priceless… go ahead and take whatever you want my guests.'

There was an abrupt rush to take anything from the house. There was a stampede and people removed all materials from the house. They carried away the furniture, roofing, brickworks, sinks, bathtubs, taps, and all that was left was the foundation which too was dug out and taken away.

The doorframes were removed, the floorboards and carpets were all removed and all the woodwork was removed and there were scuffles which broke up. Nalukuli, Mr Batwala's wife, realised that people were removing things from the house that she had to interrupt in the frenzy which was taking place as she intercepted people, demanded that she inquire from her husband about them taking away the goods.

'Why are our guests taking away our house and property?' Nalukuli asked.

'I have told them to take away anything they want from our house. We have free air to breathe, we shall live by the fresh air which isn't priced.'

'Our guests are robbers; why don't they build themselves up and wait for our house. I hope by you giving them the house makes you a man,' Nalukuli said, 'Where are we going to live with the children? Will all those who have taken over give us shelter and remember how kind you have been to them?'

'Don't worry.'

'We are homeless my husband.'

'I bought a mud hut and wattle hut that will be our home. I wanted to live as the poor and to tell the world how generous I am.'

'That does not make you a generous man.'

Mr Batwala spent the night in their new home to the disgruntlement of his family. In the morning, there was a fishmonger who sold fish on his bicycle and he was calling and summoning on buyers who were in their homes. A few people filed on around the monger and were checking the quality of the fish.

'Fish please, really fresh fish. Fresh from lake Victoria,' said the fishmonger who was screaming as he peddled around the slum.

Kamuta and Mukata, Mr Batwala's children, came out to buy fish having been given money to buy fish. They shouted to stop the fishmonger from departing before they could lay their hands on fish. They ran a short distance away after little sprint. Nalukuli told Mr Batwala to go out and look for work. Mr Batwala was given a newspaper by Nalukuli to look for work. Mr Batwala went out to look for work. He met a peanut trader who balanced the nuts on his head and he lowered the basketful of peanuts which he sold and many other children stood still around wishing to sample the peanuts yet they had money but were hungry and wished to savour the peanuts. The trader had a measuring spoon which each cost or was priced. Mr Batwala pressed ahead through the crowd to buy peanuts.

'How much does each spoon cost?' Mr Batwala asked.

'It costs fifty shillings,' replied the trader and other customers spoke out at the same time.

Mr Batwala ate the nuts which he had paid for and he walked in the streets while munching the peanuts. He passed empty shops and all trades to man were being performed in the streets which were bustling with sounds of haggling, people exchanging money and many were occupied by the day's work. Ahead of Mr Batwala was the taxi park which was surrounded by shops, cafes, and shoe-shiners. As Mr Batwala approached the taxi park, he heard a loud noise emerging which was deafening and he could hear clearly "thief", and he saw that the man who was being labelled a thief was being beaten by a large mob who took authority in their hands to beat the man. There were several policeman and women in the taxi park who were attending to no duty. Mr Batwala saw that there was no assistance provided to aid the injured man who was pleading for his life to little help. The police could not bother to stop the man from being hit. Mr Batwala approached a policeman who was idle.

'Excuse me police officer, I would like you to come to the help of a man being beaten and no one can help the man.'

'No one will die and the public is dealing with the man as their right.'

'But they are beating the man.'

'Do you know I can arrest you for disturbing me in my official duties and I am busy and I am attending to the job of keeping order and peace,' said the policeman.

'Help the man please.'

'I have bribes to take or look for and that case cannot give me bribes and by the way who told you to come to me to assist the man, I will definitely arrest you. Do you know that it's government policy to leave the police officers to find for themselves bribes by any means because the state has no money to give to the policemen and policewomen. Policing is not government priority in this case minor offences are settled by the long arm of the general public not by the long arm of the law there is no law or legislation regarding this case that you want me to handle. This case cannot provide for my food, clothing and to make me rich and comfortable.'

'Will God come and work for you and the state… can God be your slave and servant to provide all men?'

'I will arrest you I am not God.'

'Who will help the man,' Mr Batwala said.

'No one can. Let me tell you the truth and a fact. I used to be a goat thief in my village and no one knew that I was a goat thief when I enrolled and was later enlisted in the force and no one vetted my qualifications and I graduated with flying colours. I wanted to be a policeman in order to make quick money from taking bribes, by making fictitious crimes against the public. It is legitimate under this state to take bribes by all means and without anyone charging you… this is due to the fact that the state cannot afford to pay us a decent wage or salary which we have asked for. Do you understand?'

'Please help the man,' Mr Batwala pleaded.

'Therefore, I need to tell you that there is no single policeman in Uganda who could interfere in this case and I have to leave to attend to extra duties. If money can save the world, let it save a life. Any death is too much for the world and the earth loses if there is any death. What do you gain in death but with the life you gain whatever life throws at you. Death is selfish and in death there is no announcement for peace, freedom, choice, joy but it is a dark work of uneasy silence yet death is no celebration, it does not take into account the suffering and joys of life that God provided you in life. It is better to be punished in life than face death by any means. You cannot provide for yourself in death but with the life you have the ability to achieve anything. But with death there is no helper worthy of assistance, with death the world weeps over death. Any loss of life brings anguish, pain and sorrow to many loved ones. In life brings happiness which death wants to claim. It is better to be poor but have an everlasting life with no tears of anguish. Death is worse than torture, poverty and death does not mean that all is over and who knows what lies in death, the hidden problems of death are never revealed but kept under wraps that is the complete silence of death. I have for the virtue of life decided to give you all my wealth to save the man,' Mr Batwala said in a soft voice.

'That is good,' the police said.

Mr Batwala reached out of his pocket and removed a wad of notes and gave it to the policeman.

'In death you never know what you require but your requirements can be met in life and death does not own anything, but all is like how one was born going without owning anything.'

'Thank you for the bribe, I shall intervene on your behalf.'

'Life is harmony, profitability, suffering, joy, and death is hell… where there is earth, there must be heaven to support earth and because of that support and assistance, God will assist man eventually at the close of the age,' Mr Batwala said.

'How does Heaven assist and support earth?' the policeman asked.

'Look at the world, nothing would grow on earth without the rain and sun which sustain the world. The garden of the world would not grow but would remain still. With God's breath is life that each man has and without that they would not be life and we grow old due to the power of God. God preserve life till a long time.'

Mr Batwala rushed towards the scene of where the pickpocket was writhing on the ground, with a crowd which was beating him. He was helpless and he had no defence but was isolated and unable to plead for his life and the crowd was yelling and denouncing the man and all people blamed him for all their suffering. Many people had gathered around the pickpocket and all work in the taxi park had ceased to listen to the judgments of the wise public. The pickpocket sustained multiple injuries and was lying in pain from his injuries. Mr Batwala approached the pickpocket with the policeman who was more concerned with counting the money he was offered than to deal partially with the pickpocket. Several people claimed that the pickpocket had thrown away the money he had stolen to his accomplices who were at large. Many people claimed that they had seen him deliver the money he had stolen to his accomplices. They claimed that they saw him prowling around the park for victims, yet no one could ascertain his true identity.

'Why have you beaten the man and what crime has he committed?' Mr Batwala asked the crowd.

'He stole money from me,' a prostitute said.

'Does he deserve to be beaten?' Mr Batwala asked.

People had ceased to beat the pickpocket when they saw that there was a policeman present. The policeman began his initial investigation and he had never undertaken such duty. The case brought unforeseen situations and circumstances. The policeman knelt down to ask the pickpocket about stealing money from the prostitute. The policeman began his interrogations.

'Why did you steal the money?'

'I never stole any money; it could be somebody else or mistaken identity.'

'Why does the general public say you stole the money?'

'I was free, walking when it was claimed that I stole money but I haven't got any money from anyone.'

'Who should we believe that stole money from this prostitute and is it true that this man stole the money,' Mr Batwala asked the general public.

'He stole my money, fifty thousand shillings,' said the prostitute.

'Everybody saw this man steal the money,' one onlooker said. 'Where are all the witnesses to prove that this man is exactly the pickpocket?' Mr Batwala asked,

'Check his pockets,' many requested.

The policeman took out a notebook and jotted down the evidence he had chosen.

'Who is telling the truth among you? Who among you can settle the pickpocket's account of events and how can we prove that it is the man lying here? Who among you has the kindness of God?'

'All I want is to recover my money,' the prostitute said.

'We saw him throwing to his accomplices and they all ran away, disappearing into the wider world and they are at large,' many people said.

'Why do you allege he stole and you have hit him and yet you did not apprehend his accomplices?' Mr Batwala inquired.

'Check his pockets; we are definitely sure he has it in his pockets,' many people said, moving around in circles near the pickpocket.

'I will check his pockets and if I find any money I will arrest him,' the policeman said.

The policemen checked the pickpocket's pockets and could not find any money but the only thing they could find was peanuts. He continued to search the whole body but came up with nothing significant. People were astonished and disturbed as the policeman couldn't locate the money. People debated about the scene which had exonerated the man who was lying down in agony. Many people were expectant that money would be found to implicate the man and establish his guilt.

'Who will give back my money?'

The prostitute sobbed and was comforted by bystanders who cursed the man and spat on the man for his disgrace and dishonour and they were all certain that the man had brought shame to his home, his family and also to his mother.

‘I have no money but someone else stole the money not me. I was walking when everybody picked up on and accused me of stealing money.’

‘Are you sure that this man here is the one who stole the money? I want to establish the truth that he is not the wrong fish caught in the fisherman’s net and that it is not the wrong fish,’ Mr Batwala inquired.

‘He is the right fish,’ many people stressed.

The investigation had come to an abrupt end and no one came up to prove that the pickpocket had stolen the money and the policeman suggested that he should take the pickpocket to the central police station for further investigations. The pickpocket could not walk because of the injuries he had sustained. The pickpocket was lifted up and assisted carried by some members of the public. Mr Batwala made it a point to follow the procession towards the police station. The police station was nestled on a small hill, on a side stood the courts of justice, a bookshop which seemed as if it had served its time. A small square park where some people took a rest and took shelter under the trees due to the sun. Mr Batwala carried the pickpocket to the station, at the station criminals were being escorted out and inside the police station and they were all on handcuffs. Some prisoners were being transferred to prison. There were flights of stairs as one entered or came out of the police station. Some police cars and vans were in the car park. There was a harsh policeman behind the counter and at the reception and he was heavily drunk and he was scribbling notes and he was sipping his drink on duty, he was called commonly as chai because he was tough and uncompromising when unleashing punishments on criminals who were brought to him. He was fond of taking bribes and he could release any criminal until they had paid the last cent in their possession. Many people bought him drinks to befriend him in case they had to answer charges so that he might let them off. Mr Batwala, the policeman, the pickpocket and the prostitute emerged into the police station with other men who had carried the pickpocket, stepped into the station. Inside the police station were some CID offices with policemen behind their desks taking notes, conversing and laughing and typewriters were chiming away, some officers were smoking yet some were reading newspapers and exchanging words that were in the papers. There were some prisoners who were placed in jail or in cells. Some were led out yet others were being brought in; some were on remand yet some of their relatives were on hand to help them out of their predicament and plight which they couldn't free themselves easily. Some relatives spoke of bribing the officers to release their loved ones. But they were unsure how and who to contact to free them. On arrival at the police station, the pickpocket was forced to remove his shirt, remove his shoes and all his valuables and made to sit down on the floor. Further investigations were needed and the pickpocket was beaten again without any favour. He was being beaten by policemen who wanted to force out information from him.

'Who is this man?' the police drunkard asked.

'He is a suspected pickpocket and I believe he stole money from this prostitute,' the bribed policeman said.

'Why and where did you steal the money?'

'No one has proof that he stole the money only peanuts were found on him and no money was found on him. He is not a pickpocket, please chai beat him to make him admit that he stole the money,' the prostitute said.

'I have no money to show you. I am innocent.'

Chai beat the pickpocket who collapsed and there was a commotion in the police station. News spread fast that a man had collapsed to the ground while being interrogated. This news spread to news organisations who were constantly chasing police brutality on a number of occasions. News journalists came to the central police station to report the events that had surfaced and broken to the media. The general public gathered at the police station to witness on the situation that had gripped the nation. Meanwhile the police chiefs fidgeted and tried to curb any news spreading further.

'Who was responsible for this man's collapse?' one police chief asked.

'It is Mr Batwala who beat this man at the taxi park,' the bribed policeman said.

'I saw him this man at the taxi park,' said the prostitute.

'I didn't beat this man. I asked you to come to the help of this man. Didn't I? I never beat anyone,' Mr Batwala said.

'You will be charged with public misconduct for bringing the police to disrepute... Do you understand?' the same police chief said.

'I am innocent.'

Mr Batwala didn't feel like mentioning the bribe he had given to the policeman because it could bring him into trouble and he would be considered as a lawbreaker and one who was guilty to face up to his crime which he hadn't committed. It was illegal to bribe and people bribed the police under strict unknown terms which were not clearly established. It was not official to bribe the police. Anyone caught bribing would face a jail term. Mr Batwala was handcuffed and taken to Kira Road Police Station. The pickpocket was taken to Mulago Hospital. No one came to assist Mr Batwala. Mr Batwala's kindness had led him into hot soup and trouble. Mr Batwala knew that his wife and children would complain that he had let them down that he had given away the house and now that he had given away money to assist another man. They would be impatient for his wastefulness which was unprecedented. Yet Mr Batwala knew that no one could save him from this terrible situation, had come to torment Mr Batwala. Mr Batwala knew he had to face the world as a strong man. Mr Batwala knew that he was to be punished and that no one could come to his assistance. He regretted the corrupt official yet he was helpful and convinced that he could come to no harm, he would establish his innocence in court. Mr Batwala was determined to lead a good life and he had learnt a lot. Giving and receiving nothing.

Chapter Four
Kira Road Police Station

Mr Batwala was placed in prison in Kira Road Police Station. The prison was overcrowded, prisoners were standing with nowhere to sleep or rest. The new prisoners stood while old and senior prisoners had space to rest or sleep. The senior prisoners took turns to rest and command the new prisoners who were herded into crowded places in jail. The new prisoners served food, looked after the old prisoners. The prisoners had nowhere to help themselves only helped themselves in improvised buckets of urine and faeces. These buckets were held by new prisoners. The old prisoners had favours and they had unequal rights from other new prisoners. The old prisoners were allowed out to have fresh air which they enjoyed. Some times on different occasions they were allowed to visit relatives and to spend some time with loved ones. The cell was gloom! Melancholy, cold and dark with no light and the only light came from small ventilators and no one could see another person because it was severely dark. Some prisoners had gangrene, fatigue and serious fever to which they received no treatment. Mr Batwala was made to carry a waste disposal bucket of human waste. The cell was meant for two prisoners but it had more than a hundred prisoners and it was suffocating, and breathing was difficult and hampered by the serious and severe conditions which were depressive. Mr Batwala did not complain about carrying the bucket of human waste. He was not paid for any of the services rendered. Mr Batwala contacted his wife by writing to brief her on his situation which she had no knowledge of.

Dear Nalukuli,

I am here in Kira Road Police Station detained because I was trying to help a pickpocket from being beaten to death. I considered that the pickpockets' life was in danger and I stepped in by bribing the policeman and the man turned the tables on me. I am sorry for letting you and children down for my kindness. Let me hope that the children are fine and doing well under these conditions. I must be there to help the children and focus my attention to helping them out in the childhood which they must be enjoying without losing their father. Their mother must not be left to care for them alone. We should share the task of helping them. God help them in these troubled times. I hope when you get this letter you will be able to come and see me. My kindness has brought me problems and I don't regret having tried to help a pickpocket. Let me tell you that as I left home I came across a man who was being accused of having stolen money from a prostitute who had been robbed and she came along with others when the mob beat the pickpocket. No one could help so I approached a policeman who was idle and I bribed him to end the torturous beating the man was facing. However, as investigations continued at the central police station, I was held responsible for the pickpocket's collapse. I was charged with public misconduct and I want to assure you that I will vigorously clear my name from all false charges brought against me. Please, could you pass on my greetings to the children?

Yours kindly

Mr Batwala

The following day, Mr Batwala met Nalukuli who came with fresh clothes and food. She gave him rice and meat. Mr Batwala spoke apologetically to his wife in order to forgive him for his poor judgment which had landed him in trouble.

'Why do you have to be kind to the world as if the world offers you a living? You should not be extravagant,' Nalukuli complained.

'The world needs kind men like me to function and to create peace in the wider world.'

'What has your kindness brought to you? Why should we suffer for the rest of the world yet let the world won't help us first?'

'I am kind.'

'You are now in prison and the world has not freed you. Who among the children of the earth has come to help you?'

'Even though the world is not kind to me, I am pleased and happy for the courage that kindness can bring to bestow on any life.'

'You are suffering. Has the world come to your help and solve any of your problems? Has anyone come to your help… one thing you gave away the house and you threw away the money that your life has suffered and gained. Ask the world to help you now and no one has turned up and it will not, that is the fact of the world. You do not know the grain of the world my dear husband.'

'I know kindness will clear my name and you will be sure that I will be a free man,' Mr Batwala insisted.

'The children miss you and they asked me where you had spent your days and nights without them seeing you. They ask me when you will be back home. Be careful.'

'Okay, I will take care,' Mr Batwala uttered.

Nalukuli left and Mr Batwala went back to his cell and as he had settled down he read about Joseph and his brothers the biblical story of Jacob's sons.

'And it came to pass when Joseph came to his brothers, they stripped Joseph out of his coat of many colours that was on him. And they took him and cast him into a pit, and the pit was empty. There was no water in it. And they sat down to eat bread and they lifted up their eyes and looked and behold a company of Ishmeelites came from Gilead with their camels bearing spices and balm and myrrh going to carry it to Egypt. And Judah said to his brothers what profit is it if we sly our brother and conceal his blood. Come let us sell him to the Ishmeelites and let our hand be upon him for he is our brother and our flesh. And his brothers were content. Then there passed Midianites merchantmen and they drew and lifted up Joseph out of the pit sold him for twenty pieces of silver and they brought Joseph into Egypt.'

As soon as he had finished reading, there came a flood which caused the prison to flood and all prisoners escaped and Mr Batwala did not abscond but remained alone in the flooded cell. Many people came to the jail about the disappearance of prisoners and Mr Batwala was accused of calling on God to flood the prison. Murderers, thieves and all major and petty criminals were released but absconded from justice and imprisonment. Mr Batwala was accused by the general public of releasing prisoners who had let go by him and they were victims of crime and wanted justice which had now come to an end. Mr Batwala was handcuffed and taken from Kira road police station to court to face charges of releasing prisoners. Many people came to attend the trial of Mr Batwala. Most people carried weapons of violence which included clubs, batons, axes, machetes, knives, spears, spikes, bows, guns and pistols and they waved these weapons against Mr Batwala. They sang songs of war, marching from one end of the court to the very edges of the city. They danced to bring justice to the city, yet all problems were blamed on Mr Batwala and people stamped their feet on the ground and sang songs to bring a jail and death sentence to Mr Batwala. They all wanted to kill Mr Batwala. The trial of Mr Batwala was well announced just like all world trials which had come to trouble the world. The trial was well covered by the media. The media took up positions to report on the trial. But Mr Batwala sat down calmly and was silent waiting for the trial to begin. He was reading the bible and all by means his hands were in the hand of God. Mr Batwala was confident he could clear his name and that he would be free on a day and he did care about the violence outside court. A violent crowd jostled towards the entrance of the court which was sealed off by a police cordon.

'You must put Mr Batwala on a firing squad,' said one woman.

'Put him in sulphuric acid,' shouted one man who urged on people to act.

'Release our loved ones who are in prison and let Mr Batwala take their place,' said a mother of a prisoner.

'He deserves to die by hanging and beheading or total execution,' said another old man.

'How can he release my husband's murderer? Mr Batwala should serve time and the key should be forgotten and lost,' shouted one woman.

'Let Mr Batwala be released into our hands and we shall show him what we are made of and we shall kill him and no one would come to his help,' shouted a young man.

'Let us throw him into a pit of water so that he may drown with a stone tied to his back,' said one woman.

'Never release him and give him a life sentence so that he may know light but full darkness,' one man said.

'How can he release murderers when they can strike again… we shall kill him,' a fat man said.

The crowd pushed against the police cordon but to no avail.

'I am a judge because I want money for my family… I will judge to preserve peace in society. This job looks after me and no man can take it away from me. I judge to gain publicity, fame and respect in society as the greatest judge in the land. I judge so that people may fear me. I judge to gain a great reputation. I judge according to public opinion. I am the best judge. I judge to gain wealth and to be able to afford things which I desire. What have you got to say Mr Batwala,' the judge beamed.

People were yelling in the background and the noise wafted easily through into the courtroom which was proceeding with the trial.

> 'I am Mr Batwala. I have a few words to say. How can another man judge. If we are all sinners born in sin… how can sinner's judge sinners? They would lead each other into a bottomless pit where there is no one to help or to come to the rescue, just like a tunnel with no light. It is better to be punished by God rather than die or be tortured in the hands of man. God is much more merciful and caring that he will bind man's time. It is said that the judgement you pass will be the same measure you get when you judge… meaning that each judgment you pass will be the same judgment you will receive, if a man is judged to a life sentence that sentence will be the judgment that will be applied to you. It is better that you are first judged by God before you can become a judge. What judgment you pass will be the judgment you will receive. A good judge judges the world to bring peace

rather than strife and disorder. A good judge is impartial and does not profit from his judgment but he placed himself in the position and situation from those he judges… that is justice. A judge places himself in the position of his victim. A good judge is not corrupt to inspire crime but makes the world a peaceful place to live. A good judge does not harm and does not turn his arm to taking bribes or does not accept surety for any crime otherwise he will be seen as an accomplice to the crime to which he wants to end. A bad judge causes war, chaos, instability, confusion, disturbances, and riots and causes the nation to become unsettled. A good judge heals the wounds of corruption and justifies peace to the state. A good judge is not paid for his judgments so he will receive the blessings of the nation. A good judge reconciles the victim and the accused. God is the only judge that he judges the heart and mind of man. He can foretell the judgment of a thousand years. If you are found without sin by God, then you can judge. A good judge will not punish but his judgment will be righteous… because it could make one enter the Kingdom of God… because God finds no one at fault with sin to dwell in heaven. A judge who listens to evidence and listens to witnesses and third-party evidence is an unreliable judge that is incompetent because it shows he lacks the ideals of judgment and he is not well versed in his skill and profession. A nation's peace is judged by its peace. A good judge will avoid bloodshed, hatred and corruption.

That is all I have to say.

'You have spoken,' said the judge.

'Stop speaking you criminal and scoundrel,' shouted many people.

'Mr Batwala, can you call your first witness.'

Mr Batwala was reading the Bible and he did it surreptitiously. He then stood up to call his first witness. He was booed by people. Mr Batwala called for his wife Nalukuli.

'I swear to tell the truth nothing but the truth, so help me God,' Nalukuli said.

'Nalukuli, what sort of man would describe me your husband?'

'You are a very caring family sort of man. You have never raised your arm to beat me. You are kind to insects that can neither protect themselves and you are kind to all insects to roam free for they have neither power nor wisdom but are innocent without sin… you want man to emulate the insects that you don't injure.'

'What more can you say?'

'You are a kind man and you have worked hard in your life and you have helped those who cannot find a comfortable way in their lives.'

'Did I beat the pickpocket?'

'You did not and as I said you cannot harm an insect but are compassionate to insects that can neither steal, rob nor go to war. Insects cannot judge but roam innocently. If you cannot harm an insect, why would you beat the pickpocket?'

'I told you I want to clear my name.'

'Yes, that is right, try hard. We need to settle down and we are waiting for you.'

'Thank you so much.'

'Prosecution, do you want to cross-examine the wife of Mr Batwala,' the judge beamed.

'No questions.'

'Prosecution, call for your witness.'

'I will call for the policeman.'

'Policeman, what did you see?'

'I saw Mr Batwala beating the pickpocket and I called people to come and help. I thought that the man was nearly dying.'

'Perjury.'

'Silent, I want order, Mr Batwala, let's listen to new and good evidence. You had your say.'

'No more questioning.'

'Mr Batwala, you can cross-examine the witness.'

'Are you sure I beat the pickpocket?'

'I saw you. I am not lying.'

'Judge, do you like to listen to the truth or the lies that are surfacing in this courtroom. Why can't man honour his deeds… you have no idea where the truth lies otherwise you would end the trial of acquitting me. No more questions.'

'Prosecution, your last witness.'

'Come and stand before the court.'

The prostitute swore before God.

'Who beat the pickpocket?'

'It was Mr Batwala who beat the pickpocket. I saw him with my bare eyes. I am not blind. I saw him and he is the man.'

'Are you sure it was Mr Batwala?'

'I am certain.'

'That is the end of questioning.'

'Mr Batwala, you can re-examine the witness.'

'Did you see me beat the pickpocket?'

'Yes, I did see you beat the pickpocket… I want my money.'

'What proof do you have that I beat the pickpocket?'

'I have no proof but I am certain with my own eyes I saw you, please, judge, give me my money.'

'End of questioning,' Mr Batwala urged on.

'I would like to examine Mr Batwala.'

Mr Batwala swore before God.

'Mr Batwala did you hit the man?'

'No, I did not. I am like the good Samaritan and you know it so well. How much more can I save a man and I suffer for my kindness and how much more would I face the wrath of this corrupt court that is listening to lies.'

'You are responsible isn't true?'

'You have no proof that I hit the man.'

'End of question,' the prosecutor said.

'Could all of you sum up,' the judge voiced out.

'Jury as you heard Mr Batwala must be found guilty of releasing prisoners, yet he harmed the pickpocket and he has shown no remorse but justifies his actions and he should be found not innocent of the crimes brought to this court. Please make sure you reach a good verdict,' the prosecutor said.

'Mr Batwala, sum up.'

'I am innocent, I was only trying to help and I never beat the pickpocket. No one has proof that I beat the pickpocket. Jury your wisdom will be called to mind. You must be honest and honest to this land otherwise your verdict will reveal how honest you are and this nation. Why does the judge rely on juries to have a verdict for which he cannot justify? Have juries ever saved mankind out of all its problems. I ask the jury to have a verdict of not guilty,' Mr Batwala beamed out.

The judge summed up and he concluded that Mr Batwala should be found guilty.

Jury: 'We have reached a majority decision and verdict and we have listened to truthful evidence before this court and we have found Mr Batwala guilty on all counts.'

Mr Batwala was found guilty and sentencing was deferred for another date. He was told and taken to Luzira maximum prison. He was taken into prison van which was followed by many people and they threw stones and they were yelling out abuses and insults. People blocked the van on all sides and it moved so slowly at a snail's pace and was moving at intervals. Mr Batwala was shown his cell and immediately was forced by other inmates to carry out tasks which included washing plates, cups, and he was made to clean clothes. He mopped up the cell and the prison wardens made him dig plots of land. He was handcuffed and shackled when he was led into the plots of land. Mr Batwala was made to plough the land where he was instructed to plant maize and other crops and he was told to harvest maize which was due to be collected. The guards sold the maize in the black market and took the proceeds and Mr Batwala was not paid for all his duties or none ever paid him and all his work went unnoticed and Mr Batwala knew that his time had come to a half joint. Mr Batwala received Nalukuli and she thought she had brought good news for Mr Batwala.

'My husband, our neighbours are avoiding us because you were found guilty and they are calling us nasty names,' Nalukuli said.

'It does not matter at all.'

'I have very good and exciting news to tell you. We looted goods and we have furnished our house with them.'

'You have stolen sweat of others calling it your own and how can our home be a house of thieves and robbers. Take back the things you have stolen and settle down. I shouldn't like to feel guilty of the things you have stolen because if friends ask you where you obtained the goods what would one say but only feel guilty because it is not the work of our hands. Yet we have not toiled for anything. If you don't like being made penniless, why do you like to make others penniless,' Mr Batwala said in an angry voice.

'They are good things and we value them.'

'Whether good or bad I will not allow stolen goods in my presence or habitation.'

'There was a riot and everyone was looting and everyone took what they could.'

'Take them back for our integrity and honesty is at stake.'

'When will you come home?'

Nalukuli left heart-broken and felt that she had lost a lot and she wept on the way home. Mr Batwala was pardoned and freed by his jailers and walked from prison and on his way he encountered tax collectors who demanded receipt of his tax bill which he didn't provide and he had not paid tax while in prison. The government couldn't cover his tax but felt that he was on his own.

'Where is your tax bill?' demanded the tax collector.

'I haven't got any tax bill as I was in prison and I have just been released.'

'It does not matter as you are out of prison and you can carry on with your life… you must still pay for yourself.'

'If I can't, what will you do?'

'You will be placed and taken to jail, that is all no arguing at all and there is no compromise,' the tax collector insisted.

'I have no money. I will try to raise some money from passers-by and I might succeed. I want to sell my clothes which I have here in my bag.'

'We don't care how you will raise the money. All we want is for you to pay the money you owe us.'

Mr Batwala decided that he had to sell his clothes and they were the only clothes he had in his life. He was going to sell all his possessions which he had nowhere of obtaining any more clothes. No passers-by would rescue him and he knew that the world and turned against him in his quest to find peace of heart. Mr Batwala stopped one man and he elaborated to him his plight and condition. But the man had other opinions and was not bothered by what Mr Batwala had to say.

'Who wants to buy these clothes so that I can pay my tax?'

'Put him in jail if he can't pay taxes,' some passers-by.

'Remove him from our society and isolate all our good streets,' one woman went on to demand.

No one listened to any request that Mr Batwala made. People passed him while he shouted out for help but to no avail.

'Let's go to my home to get money, my wife is at home and she will assist me in the hour of my need… God will not pay taxes for me but I will help me to be freed from your tax handedness.'

'I do not like to wait for you to pay tax and I will call on the authorities to put you back in jail. I am not playing around. Pay tax or go to jail for tax evasion.'

'Let's go to my house and I will pay you,' Mr Batwala pleaded.

Mr Batwala went to his home accompanied by the tax collector. Mr Batwala shouted in a call for his wife and he looked into his houserooms for his wife. He hunted down his wife from room to room. He asked his children where his wife was and when she would return but they didn't know where she was.

'My wife is not here so I can't pay any tax.'

'I will now arrest you.'

'My children, can you help me to find anything I can sell in the market, so that I can pay my tax.' The children showed him their pictures to be sold but Mr Batwala was angry because he was in hot waters where he could not get out. Mr Batwala searched for property. He threw things in a disorderly way. Mr Batwala picked up a broken chair that he was to sell in the furniture market but it was severely broken. He dashed into the bedroom and searched for property but was unlucky. He later entered the kitchen and looked at the smashed plates and rusty cutlery which no one would bother to buy but to get them freely. Mr Batwala thought he had struck luck when he heard a radio blaring with music and he rushed towards it and when he held it in his hands, it fell apart to shreds and shards. It became dysfunctional and Mr Batwala tried to fix it but it couldn't work in any one single moment. The whole place in the house looked and appeared like a battleground which was waged to failure. Mr Batwala heard the sound of croaking chicken in a cage outside of the house. He rushed out into the courtyard and managed to get hold of the cage which he held in his hand and it dropped and the chicken flew and fluttered their wings as they made for safety.

'We have got chicken which we can sell. Get the chicken.'

The children chased the chicken around the house and the whole house was filled with feathers and all of them tumbled about as they chased for the chicken.

'Get the chicken and chase them, hold that one, my son.'

While the son followed instructions from his father, the chicken flew away. Mr Batwala dived to get hold of the chicken but failed. Thinking that luck was on his side he dived and got one.

'I have got you and you shall not come out of my grip,' Mr Batwala rumbled.

The chicken made noise in his grip. The chicken flew out of his grip and Mr Batwala cursed the world of taxes. He tried to seal the path of the chicken and dived and got three chickens. He decided to take the chicken to Nakasero market followed by the tax collector.

'How much tax do you want me to pay?'

'I want three thousand shillings.'

'The deal is done.'

Mr Batwala bargained with the chicken trader and paid him exactly three thousand shillings which he paid the tax collector. After Mr Batwala had settled his account with the taxman, he went and returned to his house finding Nalukuli sobbing buckets.

'Why did you sell the chicken? They were a treat for children on Christmas,' Nalukuli said.

'Christmas will look after itself.'

'God had given us a gift and you have thrown it away, let Him punish you and we are going to be begging all men and women of this neighbourhood for a Christmas meal.'

'As long as I am healthy and capable, you shall not beg and you shall not go hungry.'

Chapter Five

Mr Batwala was given money owed to him by the government for his services for working on the coffee farm and he decided to return to the village of Bukuku. He returned to his farm and he felt that he should revive it to a much better standard. The farm was in the hands of the government who had taken over from Mr Batwala. In the absence of Mr Batwala, the government saw it as a going concern. The farm was poorly maintained by the government which did not carry out essential work to continue the farm. Mr Batwala went to his office which was dilapidated and ruined. Bats and other birds had made home and nests in the roofing. They had dropped their droppings on the floor and walls were smeared in bird droppings. The office reeked of a fetid smell which made breathing difficult and calamitous. The corrugated roof had holes in it whereby a deluge of rain found itself in the holes, flooding the office and the office had a pool of water which contained paper work for the farm. A filing cabinet with farm documents floated in the flood and Mr Batwala waded through the flood to get to his office. Mr Batwala decided to throw away the furniture at the edge of the farm. Where some village dwellers retrieved the furniture for their personal use, they fought over the furniture which was discarded in a hurry. They followed Mr Batwala wherever he threw away the farm goods. Mr Batwala tried to call and reinstate his workers but they refused to return back to his farm. They complained that they couldn't work for little or less money and they could be exploited for nothing. They said their work was and must be valued by the powers that may be. Mr Batwala went to Mbamba people who dwelt in the mountains and consulted them on working for him. They all agreed to work for him. Mr Batwala's former workers picketed in front of the farm to discourage the Mbamba men, women and children to work for Mr Batwala. Mr Batwala confronted his former workers by saying, 'Why do you blame when you cannot work, you cannot blame me for my kindness. You will never be paid unless you work. Idle hands do not bring wealth but bring pain and suffering to those who may be idle. Skill full hands have happiness and not sadness. Return to work and you will be comforted.'

After the day's work, Mbama asked Mr Batwala for their money that they had worked for.

'We agreed that you should not be paid but receive this Tower of London photograph,' Mr Batwala said.

'You must pay us otherwise we shall burn down the farm.'

'You must agree to the photograph otherwise no pay.'

'No.'

'You said that the Tower of London looks better than money and you wanted it and preferred it to money.'

'Can we get to the Tower of London?'

The Mbamba rioted and nearly ruined the farm yet they returned to their mountain way of life which was serene and quiet. Keeping themselves to themselves. Mr Batwala turned his house into a farmhouse, he had animals. They grazed and rarely left the house. He let goats, sheep, cattle, chicken and ducks to roam freely wherever they wished to roam. He gave them feed around the house. Sometimes he sat down to read and listen to the BBC World Service. Sometimes he negotiated the cattle, sheep, and goats yet he called them by names. He set up a shop to sell milk from the milked cows in his house and set up a butcher whereby he slaughtered the animals for beef and lamb and goat meat to the villagers. Some villagers did not have money and they wanted credit in exchange for meat and milk. They in turn gave away their children into bondage to Mr Batwala. Villagers came to Mr Batwala to buy replenishments and it was the first shop to be set up in the village. Many people couldn't afford goods and the whole village was bankrupt and he gave them credit. Many people gave Mr Batwala goods and other long-held property they had and they owned nothing. Mr Batwala owned the whole village. Whatever moved in the village belonged to Mr Batwala. Mr Batwala owned all the economic sectors and no one owned anything. No one owned any possessions. They all became slaves and servants to Mr Batwala. When people saw that they owned nothing, they went to task with or to their leaders and elders to sort the mess they had found themselves in. They complained that they had debts which they couldn't afford to pay back. The village people approached the village elders who commanded respect and awe.

'We cannot accept one man to own us and all our property. The only thing we have is the air we breathe. You must save us from this man called Mr Batwala. What gains do we have?' Baluga asked.

'What do you want us to do?' one senior elder said.

'We want you to confiscate Mr Batwala's property and also to expel him from the village,' Baluga said, he was the main speaker for the villagers. 'We cannot because he has worked fair and square for his property and wealth.'

'We are all being fed by Mr Batwala. Let Mr Batwala speak.'

Mr Batwala picked up dust and capped it in his fingers and let it loose dropping to the ground.

'Dust for dust and cent for cent… you must pay back all cents you owe me.'

'No, we shall not.'

'You cannot take away what I own and I own it legally and you will find that if I take away everything you will all feel like dying.' The elders received privileges from Mr Batwala from all his dealings and trade. They were contented with what he had to offer and with the status-quo. They had not lost anything but were glad that all was well with them.

'We have decided that Mr Batwala should have all his work established for the good of the village.'

Mr Batwala went on to take over all his property by sealing all homes and houses. He placed the signpost on doors saying: MR BATWALA'S PROPERTY, PROPERTY TAKEN AND REPOSSESSED. Mr Batwala took a carriage to load it with all his property from all homes. He took everything that could move on legs and wheels. Some people that had debts from Mr Batwala escaped to distant lands to gain respect. Mr Batwala was called by his debtors and the elders reconvened the meeting. 'If people want, they must pay back all, they must give me everything,' Mr Batwala said.

'How can we pay back if we have nothing?'

'It is not Mr Batwala's problem that you have nothing,' said the elder.

'I know how you can pay me back. Let's make a deal and agreement. You can work for me on the coffee farm and I shall not forgive you until you have paid me all my money.'

'We cannot work on the farm, too much work and little gain,' Baluga said.

'Pay back cent for cent.'

'That is not a bad idea,' said one woman.

'Give Caesar what belongs to Caesar and give God what belongs to God. I cannot compromise with any of you,' Mr Batwala said in a loud voice.

'You can all leave; nothing can be done. The solution is simple: work for Mr Batwala or you perish,' said the elder.

Mr Batwala was a well-respected man and the village loved his wisdom for a number of reasons. The village brought problems to him to be settled by him. There was a case that disturbed and divided the village. They searched for answers from God as they had consulted each person but no solution was found. They argued in bars and at leisure times but no one knew when a solution would be found. There was a man who lost his only oxen and it was his only wealth and the oxen was killed by a neighbour and this incident troubled the village community pitting one against the other. The village brought the case to Mr Batwala to solve. His wisdom was called to solve a great tragedy. There were no courts and counsellors to offer advice and no one would dare solve the problem. Many people knew that Jabula would go to jail for killing the oxen. People came to listen to Mr Batwala's judgment.

'Jabula, you deprived Musasa of his oxen. I find that it was his only property. What can you pay him if you have nothing?' Mr Batwala went on.

'I have nothing to offer Musasa but only say I am sorry and I ask him to forgive me.'

'Musasa, can you forgive Jabula?'

'No, I can't. All I want for Jabula is to pay me by any means, including a replacement of my oxen.'

'As you cannot agree on any issue, I have decided to make Jabula into an oxen to replace Musasa's oxen. You will work the land until the life of the oxen was called for, do you understand, Jabula,' Mr Batwala authorised.

'That is a great punishment,' Jabula said.

'You shall work the land for him until he is satisfied to release you. He will look after you as he looked and took care of his oxen. You will not lack anything in any way possible,' said Mr Batwala.

'I know I committed a grave crime to which I have to face up to and honour.'

'What do you think, Musasa?' asked Mr Batwala.

'It is good.'

'Do you agree to work for Musasa Jabula?'

'Yes, I do.'

'Case dismissed.'

People were astonished that the problem that bothered them had been solved and settled by Mr Batwala. Musasa thanked Mr Batwala for his judgment and great wisdom. Mr Batwala was not paid but people went ahead to settle down after what appeared to be a giant task for them. And yet again another case was brought forward to Mr Batwala to solve and this too had divided the village into two vicious, opposing groups who could not come to terms with one another. A wife was beaten by her husband and she wanted to leave him yet he loved her and regretted why he had chosen to punish her.

'You should not fight or beat any woman as they are all flesh and cannot be tried as iron is tried in a furnace of hell-fire. Do you think she is a tree that you should beat her?' Mr Batwala said.

'No, I do not think so,' said the husband.

'Do you love your husband?'

'Yes, I do.'

'Because she feels pain, anguish and suffering yet it is the same flesh as yours… as it is said a man will leave his father and mother and have another wife and they shall become one flesh. She is your flesh, do not harm her as you cannot harm your flesh and her pain is your pain. Do you understand?'

'Yes, I understand.'

'I can now return her to you. Remember that she is part of you and she likes you. You are all one and the same flesh. What you desire will be what all of you desire,' Mr Batwala explained.

'Thank you for saving our marriage,' both husband and wife said.

Mr Batwala became wealthy in all manner of things and goods. He excelled and owned the village in one way or the other. He owned all the land and became the richest landowner. He was rich in cattle, sheep and goats and wherever one watched, it was Mr Batwala's wealth that one looked at. He surveyed his wealth and took round tours to examine his wealth. Whatever activity was performed in the village was Mr Batwala's own initiative. People followed him while he surveyed the village and asked him for assistance. Some made files and queues begging and praising him for helping them stand on their two feet. People envied his wealth. He couldn't leave his wealth in the custody of anyone or any other person. He became astute at dealing with his village people. Because no one wanted to work, he threatened them with putting and placing them in jail. They all expected to work little for much pay. While Mr Batwala was resting, he saw people filing into his house. They were all starved, hungry, ragged, rough, tired and weak from poverty. They all gathered near Mr Batwala's house with their failed lives. They witnessed they had no control over their lives and wanted to have some kind of independence over their lives. They lined up as in a parade. They wanted Mr Batwala to forgive them for all their misfortune and great indebtedness.

'Mr Batwala, you own us and can you forgive us, we are yours and we own nothing but only you can save us.' Baluga pleaded.

'You decide what we can do for you and ourselves,' Jabula said.

'We are all hungry and starved and we are sure that we have turned to you for help,' Beluga voiced out.

'I understand all your problems,' went on Mr Batwala.

Some of the villagers came along with musical instruments to play good calming songs for Mr Batwala. They praised him and wished him a good life.

It was his birthday and he was feeling happy and well contented.

'Isn't said that if you cannot live with less and manage with less how can you manage a lot. Work for less now and manage for less and if the future is on your side, you will be able to manage with lots. The reason I say that is because you all looking for much and have failed to live for less. All people start living with less and even though you are brought with much, you must learn to live with less at a young, rich date and time,' Mr Batwala told the people who had gathered.

'Yes.'

'Did I come living with much in this world? I found and was brought into this world by God and I must leave it as I found it.'

'We are your slaves, do to us what you want to do us,' Jabula vibrated.

'Let me make an agreement that you retain your property and land and I have decided to reinstate all your property so that you can work for me on the farm. If the farm progresses then we all prosper. If the fortunes of the farm increases and we all have higher wages including me. Let capable hands earn there lot.'

'That is a good idea. We shall work,' many people said.

'As they say lazy hands bring poverty.'

'We are happy you have restored our property and we have all agreed to work.'

Mr Batwala was happy that people had returned to the coffee farm. He was delighted that he had settled the problems of the village. The village began to function and was also busy for all hands.

Chapter Six

At the start of the day, Mr Batwala was on his usual journey and schedule. He obtained a job as a journalist. He covered political issues and he was known by his administrators for being robust and ferociously uncompromising. Yet many journalists of the time were corrupt taking up bribes to preserve for the good image of the government and Mr Batwala opposed and argued with them over the falsehoods they aired and printed out to the general public. There came a time of judgment when a politician was faced with him deciding on who among the people of the land was eligible for funding. Yet the politician had political clout. Mr Batwala pleaded with him on who should not be left out. To Mr Batwala all concerned shouldn't be left out.

'Who has a greater need than the rest? All people are entitled to a great stipend for the peace of society. If less is provided, it causes instability, war and chaos,' Mr Batwala said to the politician.

Mr Batwala was vocal, disciplined and articulate and uncompromising in the way he covered the story. He was not biased or partial in any way. Mr Batwala revealed what other journalists hid from the public. Mr Batwala was labelled a saboteur, rebel and not competent enough to address the nation on issues of national interest. He was called a dissident and one who should be isolated. Mr Batwala was blamed for bringing the journalistic professional under disrepute and he had dishonoured the cause of journalism… for good information. Mr Batwala placed his life before his life and needs or interests and his family. Mr Batwala uncovered the reasons for limiting funds to parts of society. In one article Mr Batwala elaborated that as it stands, the government cannot give out money to the nation because of what violated the security act of the nation and Mr Batwala cited that it was for the general good for the public good to reveal the truth and it was for the general good for the public, good to reveal the truth and it was for the interest of the public to know everything. Mr Batwala was put under police surveillance and his newspaper was called irresponsible yet it was because of Mr Batwala that his newspaper sold more copies than any other national paper and more than its rivals. People looked out for Mr Batwala's article. The daily journal tried partially to defend Mr Batwala's actions which covered government corruption and misconduct. Mr Batwala reported on the opulence of government officials yet the public was suffering privation and torture. Mr Batwala came to the office of the daily journal to file a report about a politician embezzling public funds. He argued with the editor to print the article. Mr Batwala pleaded that it was authentic, down-to-earth and for the public good.

'Is one single man greater than a nation of billions who deserve to have funds but deprives the nation of wealth,' said Mr Batwala. 'Is the nation for one man or is it for all men, women, and children. Who is eligible to follow the nation? We are dissatisfied with the nation and we cannot rely on the nation. We are called to abide by the laws and regulations or legislation of the nation to be called genuine citizens. Yet there is one law for man and no law for nation or government. Yet the government flouts all the laws it sets. There is no law for the government. We are slaves of the government and we have no choice or remedy for our lives.'

'I have heard your suggestions. We shall ask the government whether you want us to print.'

'Why should we consult the nation for what we want and should print?'

The daily journal faced a ban and it hadn't dismissed Mr Batwala. The government felt that its duties were being hampered by Mr Batwala and that he should be excluded from all his duties that he held as a journalist. Mr Batwala was serving and fighting for the rights of all citizens… the true freedom for the wider world. The daily journal called for an emergency session to discuss the status-quo. They had to consider that they remain independent, free from the reins of government. They wanted to end the vicious tirade of Mr Batwala. Mr Batwala categorically refused and declined to change his behaviour. He was honest and not a corrupt journalist. A great investigator and competent as a journalist. Mr Batwala informed the daily journal for it to be neutral and cautioned the paper not be the single mouthpiece of the government. Not to follow the government as if they are angels and for it to end the paper being called the brainchild of the government. The government called Mr Batwala's reputation into question… he was said to be biased, unrealistic to being self-conceit and self-obsessed overlies and lacked sincere information about the working of government. For some reason Mr Batwala was secluded and until they had reinstated Mr Batwala because he was honest and had clean hands. The government said it would withdraw its grant to the newspaper if they give the job back to Mr Batwala. The government tried to introduce new journalistic laws to monitor what was reported by the daily journal. The daily journal was a fast selling periodical and Mr Batwala woke up before anyone and reported to his offices before dawn. He sat at his word processor to edit his report and looked for any single spelling errors and checked his grammar. He sat down to write about why the government had banned the daily journal. Which had deprived the general public of any good news, yet all news has a good and bad story to tell. All news is new News. Mr Batwala insisted on keeping with his duties unhampered and to face the government in the eye. The government banned him from carrying out his duties as a journalist. They placed the secret police to monitor Mr Batwala the government feared that Mr Batwala would expose all secrets to the general public and it would cause upheaval and could cause public disorder and riots. Mr Batwala defended his duty to report on the status-quo and to quote on the situation of government. Mr Batwala forged ahead with his report for better or worse.

Mr Batwala was called to appear before a journalist tribunal.

'We understand that you are violating the code of conduct. You have broken the rules of the trade and you should be banned from your job,' the head of the tribunal said.

'I understand that the government is unhappy about some of the reports that I have issued out, yet they are not sensational or seditious to cause any public disorder or disturbance. It is the leadership under fear of the truth. If the leadership has nothing to hide, why the secrecy?' Mr Batwala said.

'You have criticised the government not abandon its duties,' the heard of the tribunal said.

'I have seen and learnt that the government has a lot to conceal and has decided to ban us from carrying forward with our duties. There is no one to blame but the government which is there to deceive and lie that they are working for the people.'

'We are not going to allow state secrets to be in the public domain. Which could cause incitement.'

'Who are you to decide what people ought to listen to and read?'

'I call on the tribunal to adjourn for two months to reach its verdict. Mr Batwala, you must report back to the tribunal.'

Mr Batwala was on trial and he felt that it was not him alone who was on trial but the general public. His integrity was on trial as well. Mr Batwala wrote of the plight of the powerless, destitute and the squalors and all those that were marginalised by the state. He reported about the injustices meted out by the state on its citizens. He defended those in pain and offered them consolation and sympathy in order to free those that were being harassed. Mr Batwala championed the rights of all citizens and never neglected anyone. Mr Batwala continued to report on the liberties of the general public and on one occasion the government charged him for libel, unfounded fabrications, rumours and propaganda which could interfere with the prevailing peace. The government called for general elections and the process was well covered in the press and Mr Batwala reported about the eventualities in the elections. The incumbent president addressed the nation on his impending campaign.

'The health of the economy is good, inflation is down and under control and the budget is balanced and we are in the black. Our policies are reviving and improving the general condition of society. I call on voters to elect me for life as I deserve to rule for life. I am the first and I will be the last president to govern the land of paradise. I am for good and not for any bad. None of you will be left out from my decision making to reflect your needs.

'You are the nation and the nation is you, without you there cannot be any nation. I am dedicated to improving on the needs of our poor folk and their ordinary lives.'

Mr Batwala reported on all the campaign and after there was a news conference.

Mr Batwala:	Who will be appointed in your cabinet?
President:	I cannot tell you who will be in my cabinet.
Mr Batwala:	When will the next elections take place?
President:	These are the last elections as I have decided to rule and govern for life.
Mr Batwala:	Thank you president and I hope you lead us into peace and stability.

Mr Batwala decided to leave political reporting to concentrate on reporting about the social issues of the day. He was commissioned to report on the traditional day-to-day lives of the ordinary people. He wrote articles which he filed into the headquarters of the daily journal. *Evil Paradise* was his first article that was printed.

Evil Paradise

Mosha began a long journey which would take him to a land of paradise. First he had to prepare himself to throw away the past but to continue remembering it in his memory. Mosha decided to live in the land of no evils which included committing evil for evil, money, gambling and haggling, strife, unkindness, selfishness, hatred, wickedness, bigotry, racism, evil rule, dictatorship, no love of life, madness, sex, trade of all kind, witchery, guiltiness of all norms, slavery, rape and committing any sin. Mosha had worked hard and he lived on the outskirts of town. As he walked, he saw a man trading and Mosha abruptly decided to talk to him about the merits of the evils of money.

'What are you selling?' Mosha said.

'I am selling pancakes.'

'Can I take one for free?'

'There is nothing for free in this world. You have got to toil for it in sweat, tears and pain.'

'It means that we are born to toil for money and no one can avoid it in their lives.'

'That's right.'

'I am Mosha I want to get rid of money and all things will belong to all mankind for free. All patents will belong to mankind. Can money own anything or is it man that owns and not money. Money is a prerequisite to owning things… it is money that can decide. Isn't that true?'

'I know.'

'Money cannot become a product… an essential product. Can money be gold, dust, food, clothing, money cannot be rain, sunshine. Yet all these things cannot be money.'

'I believe.'

Meanwhile, the weather was fine and people of all kind were congested in the city. Yet all were busy outperforming all trades.

'Whoever sells anything to another is unkind, selfish, greedy, unwilling to share. The value of money cannot be valued… can money value one particle off dust.'

'No it cannot.'

'Why do you value money?'

'Because I need to survive.'

'Life is greater than money as money cannot give life.'

'That is true.'

'Money is just a necessity.'

'I do not love God. I only love money because it looks after me where is God to look after me.'

'Why do love money and not God?'

'Because money has let me put food on the table. I have bought clothes and I own a house all thanks to money and not God.'

'Do you know that money causes hunger and starvation?'

'How does it?'

'If you are poor and destitute and you have nothing to afford like food and clothing then the money that you don't have causes you to starve… isn't correct?' Mosha asked.

'That is true.'

'Money is a source of evil again.'

'How is it a source of evil?'

'All who commit theft, robbery are evil in search of money for various reasons.' Mosha laughed and clapped his hands. And he continued to say, 'Money is the cause of slavery… slaves are instruments of shares that assist to trade as a commodity.'

'Who gave you all this knowledge?'

'I am looking for paradise that is why.'

'What is money?'

'Money for people has a value yet it cannot value a particle of dust. Money is the earth… it is the food, clothing houses and transport. If you need all those things then you need money to buy them. Money determines what kind of life you will lead.'

'I am leading a good life because I have money.'

'Money cannot value any finished product… tell me can money become a physical product to forge iron in all its processes?'

Some people came along to buy the pancakes and they were haggling and the trader calculated his money and he was happy that he had succeeded in selling his pancakes. He had made profits. Many people were hungry and starving and they came to beg but he dispelled them.

'Pancakes are my wealth and life,' the trader said.

'Without pancakes where in God's name will you get money?'

'Why do we have to toil on earth and God lives forever?'

'Nowhere.'

'What would you become without pancakes?'

'A beggar.'

'That is the reason why I would like to phase out money. To get rid of money.'

'You cannot phase out money.'

'I am going to buy all pancakes and feed all nations freely,' Mosha said.

'Come all that are hungry and starve and take any number of pancakes that you wish to have.'

There came a throng of people who came to eat free pancakes and Mosha bought all trades known to man and everything became free. Farmers would get all things freely, without money. Mosha was the last to obtain free things and was the first to work. Mosha received around the world freely. People began receiving free goods and services. Mosha wanted evil to be vanished from around the world so that it could not surface again or raise its head. No man searched for evil and yet as we know evil cannot be killed.

Mr Batwala after writing down the article posted it to the newspaper and whatever he chronicled was well received and also much desired. People enjoyed reading what he had written down. He was a celebrated journalist who had good tidings which all were willing to obtain. Mr Batwala went out to file another report.

Report to Mankind

After a long journey, Joseh was laden with goods and was well equipped for the journey. He was not exhausted but was firm on the ground. He was not bewildered or confused. He was very wise. He came against severe heat and cold gusts of wind. He was battered by coldness and rain. There came hailstorms, hurricanes and floods against him but he did not stumble. He had his world and wanted to settle where there was no mankind. He was marooned or left alone in the open spaces. Joseh had seen many wars yet he avoided all wars. He never fought in all battles that he was involved in but only rescued and gave food and water to all who were in battle on both sides of the warring. He saved many and he became an enemy soldier. He fought with skill, gallantry and purpose. So Joseh having been marooned sought to build himself from scratch without any help from anyone. He had to tame the land and also to build it up. There was no existence of civilisation of any kind. He surveyed the land and prayed that the land should offer him all that he needed. To provide for him alone. He laid down the foundations for villas. Each villa was an office apartment. He built 20000 road surfaces and bridges. He made bricks which came out of the heated mortar. He provided his possessions which included carpentry – chairs, beds and designed rooftops. He measured the land and designed a city from nothing. He built recreational sites. Joseh was an accomplished geologist, he was skilled to survey the land. He built the city single-handed and made all provisions for himself. He was a farmer. There came newcomers to settle with him. They had nowhere to stay and he gave them all somewhere to live. He gave them keys to the houses and offices. Joseh showed his new residents where each thing would be found. He showed them sheep pen, the cattle kraal, and the den of lions all mingling together. He showed them a pack of dogs and wolves. Some of them became farmers, shepherds and all was free. They all liked their new home. They thanked Joseh for what he had done for them. Joseh took turns from teaching people and working in the fields. Joseh worked alongside the old and young yet all loved Joseh. All hard tasks proved to be nothing as far as Joseh was concerned. Joseh had many skills which included farming, agriculture, business and he was eclectic. He was a good administer and he knew all trades known to man. There was never war on the land and no one went hungry to bed. Joseh's land was a breadbasket and offered food to the rest of the earth. The whole earth wanted to settle down with Joseh and they were all welcome. Joseh became a wealthy man of all kinds, he brought happiness to all concerned and was liked and appreciated by many.

Joseh called his relatives to inform them about all his trials and tribulations in a land that had nothing. He told them how the land was untamed and wild. He had conquered and he chose this land to renew his belief in the power of man to work. Even when all the residents came, they did not like to work the land. Joseh became philosophical by teaching men, women, and children. He said that if any of the residents hated one another then it meant that they hate themselves. They should treat one another with respect and not harm or hurt anyone. He told them to preserve peace for all men. There were no rules in the land. No leaders or elders came to be or to exist. Joseh did not dictate to anyone and Joseh went on to speak about some of his beliefs:

1. The greatest of wisdom has humblest beginnings.
2. Man can never be satisfied in his pursuits.
3. Man is extravagant spending all on minerals and goods.
4. Corruption breeds theft.
5. Man fights wars because he suffers from anxiety and desperation. Yet he is also deluded and frightened.
6. To acquire is to gain and not to lose.
7. A rich man may have several servants than a poor man. Yet life is greater than riches. God is greater than riches.
8. Where there are no pastures, there dwell a few. Where there is plenty and the land being lash there dwell many.
9. Those that travel love to learn and spread the word to those that have not travelled.

10. A hunter relies on his trap but not on his willingness to hunt.
11. The poor serve the rich and the rich man provides for the poor in some of their needs.
12. It is easy to build. But takes a short time to destroy.
13. A peaceful land is much loved than the land where there is strife.
14. Where there is peace, it is more likely to prosper than cause grief.
15. A nation at war loses wealth for all is spent on the war. Yet wars are a waste of essential resources.
16. A corrupt man is not kind but selfish and self-conceited.
17. A prostitute does not love but only loves money.
18. A captive is like wealth and he cannot free himself from his sentence.
19. A wise man mourns over the privation of life and dwells upon it than a foolish man.
20. All life is from God which includes angels and all manner of life.
21. One who produces is greater than the one who receives.
22. Without a slave a slave master would have to suffer hardship.
23. A slave master cannot accept to give his position to a slave.
24. The master has no sympathy for the suffering of the slave but only minds his life.
25. Slaves are like oxen and are deprived of their liberty and freedom.
26. A skilled slave will have peace of mind.

Mr Batwala filed in his report and he was confident that people would learn one or two things. He was not scared of filing his issues or articles of interest. Meanwhile, Mr Batwala sat in his journalistic office and dispensed news which was unheard of in his joint. He took to drinking tea at half break. Mr Batwala was glad that his articles were well searched for and were popular in some way. Mr Batwala sometimes was seen discussing with his editor and they were asking him questions about life. Mr Batwala claimed that it was personal but was more interested in the life of all men, women and children of the land.

Mr Batwala told them he was more likely to set up his own paper to report against the government. Mr Batwala went ahead on his typewriter to write comments and criticisms about the government. Mr Batwala sat down to read other foreign journals which reported about the life of their land. He was confident that he would leave the land if his work was curbed. Mr Batwala told his newsmen that he was a leader of the coffee farm and told them of the difficulties of working on the farm. He told them he had to rely on the news radio for coffee prices in a foreign land called Britain who dictated the coffee prices. Mr Batwala told them that it was vital for the nation to determine their prices rather leaving the whole foreigners to set the price because they would offer good prices to those that work the ground. Mr Batwala spoke of the priest Father Motala who wanted to change the behaviour of his workers. He spoke of how he missed his wife in the village and he said she was looking after the farm. Mr Batwala spoke of the need as a journalist to report without bias or partiality, to give people news about the state of the nation. Mr Batwala sat down on his desk scribing and perusing through news and he walked out of the office to go and search for more stories. He took along with him his camera to take pictures of the scenes he was to report about. He went on to develop pictures of the newsreel which he had submitted. He developed pictures of Mosha and of Joseh.

Chapter Seven

Mr Batwala had settled down to begin a life of peace. He became a peace activist and had taken time to read all books of peace. He was a very humane, sincere and considerate man. However, a lot of things happened in his time. He volunteered to welcome people in our small town. He stood at the gateway to welcome shepherds and their flock. But some people were against that to allow shepherds to dwell among them. People demonstrated against the newcomers. Mr Batwala was there to calm tempers and anxieties. He wanted people to reconcile and settle down. As Mr Batwala attempted to calm both sides, he remained focused and undisturbed but was confident of achieving an amicable result and outcome.

'We don't like those shepherds in our land,' many people yelled out.

'There is neither grazing land here and even no home or shelter for shepherds,' said others.

'We can't settle with shepherds unless if they can give us all their sheep,' some argued.

'I am Mr Batwala, did any of you create land? Wasn't it God who created land for all of us to use equally and not to segregate ourselves? We should share this land among all of us.'

The crowd grew more hostile towards Mr Batwala. The crowd took up hostile positions and demanded that even though God had created land he chose Jews to have the Promised Land, so it is wise that we have our own promised land.

'We are good and peaceful shepherds, we want you to give us a small place to graze our sheep,' said one shepherd.

'You must pay us for settling on the land,' some ventured to say.

'Was God paid a coin for creating the land? If he was paid, why should we follow the same path and wouldn't that be more agreeable to all concerned. Why are you so anxious, my countrymen?'

'There was no cost for creating land,' many people replied.

'Let's welcome the shepherds into our land and let no one have a grudge. Do you welcome them?'

The crowd debated about what to do with the shepherds. They fought that they should share their so-called promised land with the shepherds.

'We must count all heads of sheep otherwise we can be overwhelmed by them,' some insisted.

'Why number the sheep when you cannot number the dust and sand of the sea,' beamed Mr Batwala.

'We want to know the numbers so that we can plan ahead.'

'Can you number the days and nights before and after your life? Why fear the numbers… leave the numbers to God. Do you see how God punished King David for staging a census to number his troops?'

'We cannot number the dust in the world,' some people said.

'That is impossible,' said the rest.

'Because you have now agreed to share the land with us we have decided to give you free wool when we shear the sheep.'

'You are all welcome to settle in the land,' Mr Batwala said.

It was approaching midday and Mr Batwala ordered water for the sheep and refreshments for the shepherds. The shepherds were famished and sun-beaten, and Mr Batwala offered them shelter.

'A man who has been on a long journey deserves rest and relaxation,' commented Mr Batwala.

The shepherds had all their belongings with them and they had run out of supplies and all people offered them food.

'Mr Batwala we thank you for all your time and kindness. This is good land.

We are glad to be here,' one shepherd said.

'You are all welcome.'

Mr Batwala showed the shepherds where all the good pastures were and all the shepherds settled in well. During this time the town was divided over building a temple of God. There were people who insisted that it was of great importance for all people to contribute 99% of their income to build a temple of God in the land as it would bring people together and it would bring peace. That God would return to the land that he deserted. They said that all men, women and children should offer their labour to complete the task. The head of the town called for taskmasters to overlook the task. Mr Batwala realised that people were divided and couldn't stand for their positions. Petitions were arranged to fight against the planned scheme. Mr Batwala went ahead to clarify his positions. The head of the town was in his residence and people were demonstrating and arguing over how to build the temple. Mr Batwala appeared at the demonstration and they had appointed him spokesman on behalf of the people. Mr Batwala knew the task was hard and he had to pacify all sides.

'We have elected and appointed Mr Batwala to represent us,' most people said.

'We all agree,' others said.

Mr Batwala went into the heads' residence to settle the great dispute and mystery of the time.

The residence was whitewashed and opulent and lights glittered beyond his garden.

'Hello, Mr Batwala. I want all men, women and children to build this temple.'

'You cannot achieve that in your lifetime.'

'Why do you say that?'

'Because God has not anointed you to build a temple to represent the image of God. If he anointed you and gave you the task, then you could go ahead. The temple must be in the image of God. What I am trying to say is this: you need all the plans of the temple to be given to you by God as God wishes and with all his endorsements.'

'That is impossible.'

'You cannot know the exact imprint of the temple of God. God does not need a man to labour over his temple. His temple does not require taxes. The temple of God cannot be destroyed in the hands of man. In his temple there is no rot or rust.'

'You have a great point Mr Batwala.'

'Gods' temple will appear as New Jerusalem… where there is no filth or waste.'

'That is true.'

'The closest they came to building a temple of God was when they built the temple of Solomon even that was the work of man and also it was destroyed in the end. Yet those who destroyed the temple couldn't destroy the presence of God, a man of all generations.'

'It is sad they destroyed that temple.'

'Solomon's temple was like what man could give God.'

'I have decided to give up on the temple of God.'

There were jubilations that all plans to build a temple of God had been shelved and all people welcome the wise decision not to go ahead with building the temple of God. People went back to their work and returned back to their lives.

There came a time where many people fought over the single well that provided fresh water for all. The weak couldn't draw water. They had to wait for several days without water. They prowled for water but with little success. Those that were rich paid in advance and obtained water at ease. The shepherds found themselves without water for their sheep. It reached a point where people found out that the well was beginning to give up. The water eventually gave up. They called Mr Batwala to improve the situation.

Mr Batwala approached the strong men who had stopped the well from providing water. The strong men had run out of options and had failed to come to terms with the prevailing situation. Mr Batwala called the men, women and children to the only well that provided water so as to assess the situation which had gotten worse with time.

'Who dug this well?' Mr Batwala asked.

'No one.'

'With the hand of God it was formed, it was through him that it came to be and no one among us has ever formed any well. Let us bless God for what he has done for us. To form this well.'

'We want water. It's drought and no water is available,' some people ventured.

'With the blessing of God we shall have water,' said Mr Batwala.

'Why do these men stop us from drawing water from this well? Did God create the well for only them and their sheep? Where they in the mind of God to create this single well from us? Did God forget us in his mind, to go out without water?' said one woman.

'You men, you were responsible for forming this well?' Mr Batwala asked.

'No, we weren't.'

'Each person has a right to draw water from this well. God never created this well for only you. For God gave the well that we should share it and you have dictated that no one should stand before you to draw water.'

All people agreed to use the well and share it properly and with no conflict of interest involved they all said that the little water that was available they should try and share. They were all glad and elated with excitement and joy. The strong men regretted and felt sorry for causing misery knowing that they were acting selfishly in the way they were using the water. The strong men apologised and denounced the way which had brought suffering to many people. They declared that they would share the water and make sure that the well would not give up.

'Water doesn't select who should use… it is humble and it's for everyone. Did this water select you to use and did it deselect those who you have stopped from drawing water?'

'No, it did not select us.'

'Is this water against those who you had stopped from drawing the water?'

'Drink this water all of you and I will speak with my mouth,' Mr Batwala asked.

Mr Batwala drew a little water from the well and gave it to the people who wanted to draw the water and they all tasted it.

'You have all drunk the water.'

'Yes, we have.'

'Is the water against any of you?'

'No it isn't.'

'Does the water kill, hate or discriminate against any of you that you cannot use it?'

'No, it does not.'

'You should not turn the well against anyone. Has the water dictated that is only the strong ones who have to use it and not the weak?' Mr Batwala asked.

All people agreed to use the well and to share it properly and not to cause conflict among themselves. The strong men agreed to use the water without stopping anyone from using the well. They had averted war and strife. There were celebrations which took place whereby people were dancing and singing. Peace returned to this small town.

The town was large and it was able to hold a great number of people. But there came a flood of immigrants to settle in the town. They were placed into refugee camps because people were afraid to welcome them. They were given meagre food parcels which were not enough… the conditions of the camp were like pigsties. The immigrants never revolted or rioted. The refugees were running away from wars. The immigrants came from corrupt countries and they were running away from wars. The immigrants were happy to be in the camps rather than take liberties in their own countries. The townspeople branded the immigrants liars, thieves and economic refugees, cheats who came to rob the town and take all work from the town people. The townspeople rioted against the refugees and wanted to send them away. Mr Batwala intervened.

'You know in some countries people were immigrants before and they formed nations yet they now disallow foreigners from settling in their land. No one has a birthright to his land… it belongs to the whole earth yet all that is here is for the Almighty God. Has the land claimed that you own it?'

'We don't want foreigners,' said one man.

'We must allow people to settle in this town.'

'Who will look after them?'

'We must allow people to settle. They shall give us wealth. The more the people, the more the wealth that they will give us.'

'Whole we are saying is that our land should not be given to foreigners. We shall have nowhere to stay. Save us from these migrants God.'

'When our ancestors came home, they claimed the land yet they had come from afar and they were not stopped from occupying the land. They built up this place and so we should allow others to settle in the land. You shouldn't feel anxious and worried of people coming here to settle. Take care of yourself and the land and God will take care of the land,' Mr Batwala said in a calm voice which appealed to many.

'Can we allow them to settle,' one old man intervened.

'Many heads are better to solve a task that has defeated the few heads. Will tell you a story: there was a man who was rich and he was a farmer. He worked the land alone and the land was in a fallow and he cleared the land to sow wheat. He went ahead to clear the land and he sowed. He harvested his crop and he had to market his crop yet he was overworked. Yet he realised how hard and difficult the task was before him. He couldn't handle the task single-handed and he faced problems. Yet failed to carry out the task alone and he abandoned his task and spent all his wealth. Yet if he had extra help and labour, the task wouldn't be as hard as he thought. He ran out of money and mourned for his loss. If he had extra help, he would be content and satisfied. Because he was alone and hadn't called for extra help he suffered a loss. Therefore, allow people to settle in the land and you won't regret.'

'Okay, they are welcome to settle in the land.'

'Has God ever banned a single person from dwelling in a land of his choice? This town has set up boundaries to limit its expansion yet God has not placed any boundaries to prevent us from occupying the land. All streets have a beginning and an end. All life has a beginning and an end. All pain has a beginning and an end.'

'We all have seen the advantages of welcoming people to settle in the land,' some said.

'They are all welcome to settle in our land,' said all.

People were simply disturbed to hear the news that the newcomers had a different language and came from a different tribe. They wanted to expel and deport them because they feared that they would overwhelm them with a different language which had a different tradition. Mr Batwala was called to intervene. The town people felt that they should teach the people their own language so that they may settle in well.

'I am Mr Batwala, all languages came about from the Tower of Babel. All languages have the same disciplines of meaning and intention. They have similar ideas and ideals which can be known by status and tradition. All languages have similar cooperation of thoughts and behaviour and characteristics which are identical. The Tower of Babel created differences and but people could still communicate. There are inhibitions with languages but that has not stopped people from communicating. People have different speeches about the same things… take for example things like money, children, clothing, travelling, love and hate, leadership, walking, running and so many other things that one can imagine. They all exist in all languages. All languages speak of the same things and all possess ideas,' Mr Batwala said.

'We cannot understand what they are speaking about,' said one woman.

'You must accept to leave and make a disadvantage into an advantage. Let's allow them to live among us.'

Mr Batwala wrote a letter to his wife and he explained to her that he was busy. He wished to know how the coffee progressed. He felt that it was important for him to change jobs to acquire skills and to get away from the village of Bukuku which was unstable. Mr Batwala wished to have some bit of independence and not to isolate himself but to continue his work which did not bring him in conflict with his workers. Mr Batwala was tired of arguing with his workers but felt it important to be a human rights activist. He was not seeking popularity or any undue gain. He was focusing on his new duties which took him from one place to faraway places and land which he had not visited before. Mr Batwala spoke of his life in the town and spoke of his undying love for his wife. He sent them money to pay the workers on the farm. Mr Batwala was working to improve on the conditions of the farm. He had to save for some reason which he never knew but was aware that he was comfortable and safe. Mr Batwala took his time to study the ways of man and prayed that God would give him a life which he sort. There was no time to waste and there was no time to relax. He offered his ideas and beliefs to all concerned. He had to toil because God wouldn't come to work for him. He had to help himself and God would assist him in the end. Mr Batwala was a bit anxious about the way the farm was set up and organised. He felt that the workers would desert the farm and leave him without any income. He knew he had settled the issues and problems which belied on everybody's minds in the village. He knew he needed the people and workers to work on the farm. He was deeply dependent on them and they were in turn dependent on him. He felt that he should not desert them but he felt he should assist them where possible. Mr Batwala continued to follow the coffee prices on the BBC World Service. The news came in as follows: 'The coffee prices per tonne are as follows, one tonne of coffee is two hundred pounds. We advise people to continue planting coffee.

There is a glut and major producers of coffee have cut down on their coffee.'

There were food shortages and people were hungry. They began to demonstrate over food supplies. People were hoarding food supplies and people were confused over where the food had disappeared. Shop owners were charging exorbitant prices and people couldn't afford the prices of food. People began searching for food. Whenever they went customers were told that there was no food. They were bewildered over the lack of food. They blamed the shop owners for the shortages. The people decided to take the law in their hands in order to find out where the food shortages had originated. Mr Batwala was called to calm the situation.

'I am Mr Batwala, no one has a right to hoard food to push up prices. We need to supply food for all. Do not hoard food. There is plenty to go around and there is no need to hoard,' said Mr Batwala.

'We must hoard and you cannot end this situation,' said one shop owner. 'We shall call for other towns to supply food and we shall ask our farmers not to supply you with new supplies unless if you can stop hoarding the food. People would buy directly from the farmers,' Mr Batwala said.

'Please, Mr Batwala, do not do that. We are shop owners and we need agents who take the whole lot out of our income,' said one shop owner.

'We shall reconsider our position,' said one shop owner.

'You have an option to sell food to all customers. If God did not create food, where would the earth be? A good trader is one that does not look to exploit another customer. A good trader accepts credit with no interest. A good trader does not withhold his hand to serve, a good trader is sincere and truthful and offers. His services with care. A good trader cuts or reduces the prices of his goods in nothing in return. A good trader does not accumulate credit from the customer in order to gain interest. Serve with one heart. A good trader serves with one heart no thinking of gaining and loosing which is two hearts,' Mr Batwala beamed.

'We are corrupt traders,' Mr Batwala said.

'God employs the world. He has employed you to serve yet you don't know.'

'How does God employ the world?'

'He created the food which you are selling. If he hadn't created the food you would be without a job. God employs the farmer and baker of bread… from a wheat farmer to a bread baker God employs all yet he receives no money.'

'You are right. We shall be honest for the good of the world and all our efforts shall serve the world,' one shop owner announced.

'Fear God for what he can do. God can send one to hell and another to heaven. For whatever you do is bound up in heaven or hell. The choice is yours.'

'We shall turn our hands to perform what is correct and good in God's eye. We have done what is abominable in God's eyes. His judgment is before us now. What can we do to be good in the eyes of God?' one shop owner interposed.'

'You must reach out to do some good even when you are poor, you should live as a rich man. Comfort one another,' Mr Batwala responded.

The status-quo changed for the better. The shop owners agreed to end hoarding. People gathered to witness the speeches and they followed what was being recommended to end the predicament which had troubled the community. They were satisfied with the outcome. Some were yelling in happiness and they went out to buy whatever they desired. The traders reduced their prices and gave all the food to eat. All town folk came to listen and they were hungry and hoped for free food which was aplenty. They queued for food and never fought and there were no scuffles but people shared food which they had received. There were all different commodities which were being sold to the town folk. People lined up for food in long queues until nightfall. Some people sold some of their mementoes, jewellery, furniture, bedding, clothes, cutlery and all other personal possessions which they did not value in order to buy or purchase food. People bought food in large quantities because they feared that the town would run out of supplies. They knew that whatever they bought would last for a lifetime. There was no ration in any way. Each person bought goods which they thought would suffice.

'You must end buying food in large quantities. There is much to go by,' some shop owners said.

'You must not dictate to us. We are not a nanny state,' said one customer. 'We need to stock up on food because food would run out,' some people said.

There were hawkers who haggled over the prices of their food. They created a situation of scarcity and made customers to panic. People bought things from the hawkers. Some customers bartered with the hawkers and felt that they were being duped into buying food because there was nothing. Yet another issue arose about land reform. There was a man who was in a commune. He wanted to buy land away from the landlord. The landlord sold his land to his squatters who paid for services for using the land. As such a conflict arose that pitted the landlord and his workers. The landlord felt that he should sell his land to the man. The squatters complained to the landlord that they had nowhere to live or work the land. They said he wanted to deprive them of the land. The man who wanted to buy the land informed the squatters that they should destroy all their homes and all their property. He wanted to evict them from the land. He told them to leave with all their animals. They pleaded with the man to leave them alone and to make them use the land as before. They said they would serve him with dedication and also with respect. They offered him their wealth. But the man did not accept any of the reasons given. They could not come to an amicable agreement. The squatters were faced with an eviction order which could be enforced on them. They lamented and cried and asked God to come to the rescue. The squatters said they would pay the man some money so that he could leave them alone. The man set up a price for his conflict resolution.

'I am Mr Batwala, the land was created by God at no cost. Land should be used freely. No price should be placed on land. God never charged anyone for using the land. He offered it freely. Everything comes from land and no one can value land. Can you put a value on one single particle of dust?'

'No, we can't.'

'Everything that comes from land therefore should be available freely,' said Mr Batwala.

'What is that?'

'What would man rely on if this land was not created? Would man come up with his own ideas creating by creating his own world? Even man does not know what this earth is made of…

what is dust made? What makes of dust are there… what sort of material is the dust let alone the trees, leaves, gold and the iron itself… if man knew what make-up of material those things were made of he would recreate them rather than exploiting them. What make-up is the sun and the moon? Can man create the world, the sun and the moon?' Mr Batwala asked.

'All I want is money.'

'We should use the land freely because God has not charged us for using the land.'

'I would have liked to buy land for myself but all has come to an end,' said the man.

'Money turns hands into slavery… each person has to work for it. Money exploits and makes people into servants of money. All people have to depend on it. Yet money comes from the land. We are all slaves to land. It dictates what sort of life we can all lead.'

'That is true.'

'Despite the fact that we are all slaves to land… the land is a slave to man because it is worked and exploited to serve man. Man obtains minerals and resources from it and everything has a price on its head. It is a dual slavery. It is better that all the earth should be landowners and not face the task of being landless. No one should accuse me, I am only commenting on the issues that are not explained by any normal or ordinary person.'

'But you have changed the outlook of our society. You are bringing us into a strange situation. Who can end your ideas?' said one woman.

'We must take you to court for upsetting the peace of our society. We are fed up of your rhetoric and statements which have troubled us. Who can live with your ideas? We shall charge with sedition and for disturbing the peace of the land.'

'We are fed up of your ideas which put us into a difficult situation,' said one man.

Mr Batwala chose to lead the people because he knew it would bring peace. Mr Batwala knew that it was better to live in a peaceful place than live in a place like a battlefield. Mr Batwala was a pacifist and he knew that he could not benefit. He looked back at all his work on the farm, being a journalist and contributing to human rights. He knew that his ideas would bring him into conflict. Not all people would agree with all he had to share and he felt that he was driving his life into turmoil and trouble which he could not unravel. He knew he had left his wife and children in the village to look after the farm. Mr Batwala liked the experience of working in different situations. He was not hiding away from his farm duties and also from his wife. He desired order and he had established in society. Mr Batwala was very angry with people who wanted to put him in court. Mr Batwala wished to learn from his past and called on his experience which had led him to this part of town, Mr Batwala never shied away from any decision making. Mr Batwala was committed to look after the farm, he wanted to expand on his interests and he believed in the power of will. Mr Batwala was alone and he could not rely on himself. No man could come to his assistance. He was alone and isolated, the isolation was not definite. He knew that he could call for trouble in one way but he only had to wait patiently.

The people were annoyed and disturbed by Mr Batwala that they committed him to face trial by any means possible. Mr Batwala was confident that he would overcome all obstacles, he knew that he had committed no crime. Mr Batwala resumed his wish to bring peace to the world. He was mentally focused and composed. He initiated his mind to strange ideas and beliefs that no one had. People were amazed by his ideas and beliefs which were a bit rare. Many people did not like to be told what to do by another person. They felt that Mr Batwala was like a leader in waiting and a leader who came to dictate to them. Mr Batwala some thought that he was a dictator who found it fit to rule over some ideas against them. Some people were offended by some of the ideas that Mr Batwala came up with. They felt that they or their freedom was being eroded. They would put him in court to retain some beliefs in some of their ideas. They felt that Mr Batwala was a teacher who governed with an iron hand. People didn't like to be told what to do, changing their outlook on a number of issues which bothered by the day. They recalled how Mr Batwala and his ideas had let in shepherds, immigrants, foreigners and the issues of lack of the well. They were completely flabbergasted and confused about whether to bring proceedings against Mr Batwala. Mr Batwala was called to clarify his intentions and what he meant and intended to do to the people with some of his ideas. Mr Batwala was sane and knew people would be a little bewildered and they could have mixed feelings about some of the things that Mr Batwala had to say. Mr Batwala knew for some reason that God was not on his side and all that occurred to him reflected that view. Mr Batwala had to carry on regardless. People met to discuss what to do to Mr Batwala for what he had spoken against. It seems that Mr Batwala had committed a crime of sorts against the people. They followed him wherever he went. Mr Batwala replied to his critics that if he was in the wrong and he had been communicating to them in public, why were they seeking his life. He told if he had wronged the powers that exist would have found fault with him. But all was easy for Mr Batwala was not native to know that not all people liked his views and he knew that he had dealt with a number of people to come to that conclusion. A man stands by his words and action. Whatever one says, it comes from the heart and mind. Nothing is spoken abruptly but is spoken with the desire of the heart. Mr Batwala didn't conceal any of his beliefs but intended to bring a complete understanding of the issues involved. There was a commotion in the town. That commotion came about as a result to Mr Batwala, there were two camps, those that supported and disliked Mr Batwala. Yet it was not the intention of Mr Batwala to create division among the people. Mr Batwala knew that the people did not like what he stood for. He was firm and adamant that he stood by his own ideas to improve the general condition of the community. Mr Batwala wanted to change the community for the sake of his children. He believed that it was the responsibility of everyone to improve on the situation of the day. Yet brought himself into trouble. The problem was that people never liked to be told what to do. Mr Batwala got a report from his wife that there was a rebellion among the workers. They had given up work. But Mr Batwala could not be in two places at one time but had to concentrate on one single issue. Mr Batwala felt that he had abandoned his village for a long time. Mr Batwala couldn't succumb to the idea of running two lives or to lead a double life. Many people accused Mr Batwala of public order offences. They blamed him for disrupting the status-quo. He was to be tried in court for public disorder and sabotage. Mr Batwala knew he would clear his name in any case. He wasn't timid or frightened in any case. He knew that as a matter of principle he could get on with life.

He believed that all was meant to be because of God. There were some people who didn't believe in the power of God. Mr Batwala tried to avoid court, yet the case would be in short while. Mr Batwala knew that his life was on trial. His words and action were on trial. His integrity was on trial. The world as well was on trial. The people too were on trial. Mr Batwala knew he would pay the last coin for his trial. Where was the justice to blame Mr Batwala? Mr Batwala knew that the earth is corrupt and that he wouldn't receive justice in this case. Mr Batwala knew that if justice was or would seem to be achieved then he would be freed. Mr Batwala knew that the truth would be told in court. He never gave up or in any case. People were happy that Mr Batwala was to put on trial. The trial of the world. There were people with conflicts and they settled these in public arenas. So they felt that Mr Batwala would face these arenas. They wanted Mr Batwala to fight a lion in an arena and if he wins he would have cleared his name. It was the general held view that anyone who fought successfully and defeated the lions then they were not be guilty. Many people never quite made it. But Mr Batwala was confident that he would make it. Mr Batwala went into the arena and slept by lying down silently and the lion took to smelling his breath but lay down after Mr Batwala. The lion laid down besides Mr Batwala and people were amazed that Mr Batwala had survived.

Mr Batwala was taken in to face trial. The charged him with public disorder offence. Which Mr Batwala firmly denied what he was being accused of. 'I am the judge trying this case. You are being accused of civil disobedience and sabotage, you have upset the make of this society and you have introduced your ideas which are detrimental to the peace of this land. What has Mr Batwala got to say to the charges brought forward to this court,' the judge said.

'I would like to say what crime have I committed. I have disclosed some ideas that I found to be important and vital to the general public. I stand by every word that I have said. I have not harmed or injured any one. I have spoken my heart and mind any God is there as a witness. I denounce all that is against me and a totally deny any wrongdoing. Why didn't you accuse me when I was there in public speaking about the things you are accusing me for? I have no criminal record to my name. I am an innocent man trying to save the world from walking blindly into fire of chaos and confusion. Who would want his sheep to walk in fire and not save the sheep? I have saved many and the sheep have turned around and they are accusing me of wrongdoing. Where is the justice in all that is taking place? Should I have allowed the sheep to walk blindly into the fire?'

'No shouldn't leave the sheep to walk into the fire, you did a good thing.'

'Are the sheep lost and have they perished?'

'No they haven't.'

'A good shepherd saves the sheep from the mouth of the lion just as King David saved his fathers' sheep from the mouth of the lion, if he had failed to save them the lions would have turned on him. He was victorious. I have saved many sheep and I will continue to save many sheep.'

'You are not a good shepherd to tell us how to live our lives and saying you saved us your sheep.'

'Who among you is facing trouble?'

'None. We don't like the way you have saved the sheep.'

'A good shepherd removes all pain from the sheep. A bad shepherd leads the sheep into a furnace. Have any of you gone into the furnace.'

'Try him.'

'It is better to be tried by God than by man. God is merciful and kind. He will feel sympathetic and he will feel all your pain but man does not.'

'Forget about that foolish talk about your God. Does God provide me with a plate of food?'

'Yes he does. He gave you life and that life is his not yours and you are a custodian of that life. He keeps you in one piece. Whatever you do that is God in your life.'

'It is whole your words that have brought about you being charged. You are the shepherd that revealed the wrong information to the sheep. The sheep are scattered and displaced. You have to face the consequence of your actions,' the judge declared.

'I haven't caused any strife in the community. The community is safe,' said Mr Batwala.

'You accepted the shepherds, the immigrants, well and people felt that you are trying to make lost like the lost sheep,' the judge beamed.

'I haven't made any sheep to get lost. I meant well and you have turned the tables against me.'

'You have placed yourself into trouble. Do you understand?'

'I can't accept that.'

'We wanted our Temple of God and now we having nothing. Put him in jail,' one woman said.

'If I were wrong in the beginning, you should have told me so before.'

'There was no need to tell you anything,' said the judge.

'If anything, it is not good to read into the words of God for perfection and time is the judge of all things. Who can judge God? If there is any man who can judge God, then he will be a true judge. To judge the heavens and all its host and to judge creation in all its form. For with such a judge would be how great man can stand. To judge death and the dead and living. There is no way a man can stand trial. To judge death and the dead and living. Are we all here to be judged by God in the end of time at judgment day? Therefore judge, you have not got the credentials to judge, for your scope of judging is minimal. It cannot stand the test of time. The judgment of God is forever and yours is for a sentenced period and time is of the essence.'

'Are you trying to accuse me of my work? You value my work because it is important.'

'If with your judgment you judge, then calm the situation which is impending in the community,' Mr Batwala suggested.

'I am the judge of people. I am the judge of the world.'

'How long have you been a judge?'

'For a certain period.'

'Will those you charge last for a century and millennium?'

'No they won't.'

'Man is not to powerful. He is bent on tradition and cannot change the shape and make of society. Fashion changes but man remains committed to tradition.'

'Mr Batwala, why do you want to change the tradition of this society?'

'I am not a man who can change the world. Let me tell you where I have treaded before. I was a slave, and my parents left me with money and I began to look into the world. I wanted to make a contribution to society. Or give society what it had given me. I wanted to honour the world. I set up a farm of coffee. But work was hard and found out that life on the farm depended on the price of coffee. If coffee prices were high, then people would be paid well. Which would mean that life on the farm would continue because people are paid well. Suddenly, prices were low and people refused to attend to their work on the farm. The farm provided the main income in the village and people found out that the farm provided the only work. I was desperate to find a way of price vicious circle which had engulfed me and my workers. The only way I thought was for me. I left the farm and settled in Kampala city. But I was out of work and was placed in jail where I was acquitted and returned back to the village to resume work on the farm. I am a mam with many responsibilities. I have put my heart and mind to other forms of work which include being a journalist. I want to occupy myself because farming is not a secure job at all. I am here now as a pacifist and a human rights campaigner. I am charged with a lot of duties.'

'You should give away all that you have owned to be freed.'

'How much money would suffice the charges brought against me.'

'All your earnings.'

'My world would come tumbling down.'

'When would the world stop relying on money?' Mr Batwala asked.

'I am the judge, you must take responsibility for you actions do you understand Mr Batwala.'

'Where on earth would a man have rest and be at peace with the world,' Mr Batwala mentioned in a calm voice.

'What should we do to Mr Batwala?'

'You are a judge try him is isn't.'

'I will find out what I can do.'

'Let him off,' some people said.

'There is no point in trying him.'

'What have you got to do?'

'To be calm,' Mr Batwala said.

Chapter Eight

People wanted more power and authority to run their lives. They did not know who to consult about their lives. They felt alienated and unable to participate in the political process. They felt like prisoners who had no say in their lives. They felt that laws and regulations were preventing them from participating in the political process. They knew their leaders were dictators. They wanted to fight the oligarchy which had adopted laws against them. People's lives were extremely lowered that no one had power. They could not inform their leaders about their lives. They wanted to topple the highest echelons of power. They did not have enough influence and capability to form their own laws. They were told to follow the leadership which imposed its power of them. There were twenty leaders who passed the laws. They passed the laws on behalf of the majority. Many unfair laws were passed to the opposition of the people. There were no elections to nominate the leaders. The leaders made act of laws as they felt fit. The media was state run and controlled. The media misrepresented the opinions of the people. They could not protest in any way but led simple oppressed lives. There were told to follow all leaders. People were not happy with the administration which had failed to give them power. Those that failed to follow laws were apprehended and held incommunicado in mass security prisons. The leaders tortured their own people and never released any political activists who had fought for the rights of all people. There were riots which came to resemble quagmire. There was unrest in the public brought by lawlessness. You should respect all authority as it comes from God. People felt that their freedom was being curbed and they felt unhappy about the rule of treachery. There was no one who raised their head in public. Because they feared the consequences and outcome of leading people into opposition.

The opposition was crashed by mass arrests and all dissidents were forced to abandon their protests. More people decided to leave the land to migrate to distant lands far away from the community. The leaders issued decrees and orders and imposed a curfew on the people who had brought the land to its knees. The leaders were paranoid and suffered from deep depression. There was a time of mourning and a time of laughter. There was a time of celebration and a time of weeping. A time of joy and a time of sadness. The leaders called for reinforcements to battle against the people – the protesters. There was a commotion in the land and all was not well. Public gatherings were banned.

They imposed fines if any one broke the law or violated the curfew. The leaders met in private to form the laws and legislation. Yet they had no people in mind. They went ahead to form laws as they felt fit. They never were compassionate on those that followed their laws. They led with an iron fist. They adopted laws that oppressed everyone. They were meaningless laws and did not reflect the mood of the nation. The leaders led for the sake of leading and never took account of the social implications of what their laws would provide. They came up with laws such as people should not walk in a group of two and they outlawed anyone from laughing in public. There was no one allowed at the secret meetings when the leaders were forming laws. People were *persona non gratae*. People were accustomed to the bad leadership. They were taxed for walking in public. There was silence which was observed by many people. They were rounded up for questioning by the leaders. They were taken in asked what they felt was good or bad about the nation and its leaders. The leaders banned people from praising God. All places of worship were closed down. People were put under house arrest and told not to venture out in anyway. The people were told not to buy anything for some days. The leaders spent most of their time drinking and involving themselves in orgies which lasted for years. They banned any mentioning of democracy. The people were told that good citizens abided by the dictatorial laws. They handpicked policemen and army officials. The leaders were frightened that people would topple them and they believed that insurgence would continue to spoil the mood of the time. There was a life sentence imposed on people who violated the law and flouted the law. People were adamant to a point of rebellion or rebelling against the nation. The leaders personally edited the news which people read but never believed in any way. Rumours abounded about the death of the leaders to the satisfaction of all concerned. The leaders in return banned people from working and realising. The leaders wanted the people to kowtow on all their laws which were oppressive and which were not a mirror of society. The leaders embezzled money from the exchequer and took all the resources for their personal use. People were powerless to stop the theft. The leaders used their resources which they had stolen, a complete kleptocracy. Many people were left penniless and they had nowhere to get income or finance. Many people were welcomed in underground movements. The leaders went on to ban liquor and cigarettes. Music was banned by them. People felt like they had no leader in waiting, which leader would lead them to greater things. People mused over some ideas; a man could be brought down by a quarrelsome wife and a leader could be brought down his power. No man stood alone and no nation was alone in all its struggles. The leaders decreed that people should praise them as they praise God. People were forced onto hard labour camps and they faced hardship. Many people perished on these labour camps. People lost their loved ones as they didn't know where their loved ones were taken onto labour camps. They toiled and witnessed hardship. People were afraid to talk in public about where their loved ones were. No letters were allowed onto these labour camps there was no one allowed to communicate to their loved owns. Soldiers were put on high alert on these labour camps. People worked harder than Jews in Egypt. Many people were left hungry and starving as the leaders would not provide for them. People felt that they were losing out. They lost their integrity and respect. There was no shelter on the camps and there was no one to help them in all their work. When they complained about the conditions on the farm, they were told to get back to work. People were hungry and they couldn't be saved by their own hands. Problems were resolved by fistfights. People were very angry with leaders for forcing them onto these labour camps. God couldn't come to their rescue as he helped the Jews from the hand of Pharaoh. They called on God to come to their help. To fight the evil rulers with pestilence. But nothing came to be. They wanted a leader who would lead them to safety and who would free them from the hand of the evil rulers. People were forced to buy pictures and photographs of the leaders and whoever didn't have any were arrested and some were placed onto the labour camps. People felt annoyed and they really wanted a leader to take them into good and peaceful pasturelands in a land of the living. Images and statues of the leaders were seen along the boulevards. They towered like the cedar of Lebanon. There were all camped together and were lined as if they were going to execute them. They worked under all weather conditions. Even when it poured buckets they still worked. The leaders brought in people to build them palaces across the land and all those that did build were not paid. They were all given food as payment. The labour camps were congested and spilled onto other lands disrupting the state of the nation. No one would rescue the people from all their hard labour. The leaders claimed that it was development to make people work on the land. That all those on the labour camps were idle and did not have space for them in cities. They were told to work hard to fight poverty. The principle of the objective was to make the land more organised.

Mr Batwala was called in to lead the people. He was told that it was important for him to lead the people. There was a general accepted view that Mr Batwala was the man fit enough to lead the people. Mr Batwala decided to take on the mantle. He would lead them into new pastures that were lush. People voted to make Mr Batwala represent them on all issues that troubled them. Mr Batwala first objected but gave in to the support he got. Mr Batwala went to the palace of the leaders.

'I am here to address the problems that beset the people. I want to speak to you about the state of the nation,' Mr Batwala said.

'There is nothing you can say,' the senior leader said.

'People want democracy and the rule of the ballot.'

'We don't accept the ballot here.'

'You must allow the people to express themselves.'

'Who are you tell us what we should do?'

'I am Mr Batwala and I have come here to save the people. Anyone who saves a man saves the world.'

'You cannot save the world. We are the only leaders who can save the world.'

'What ideas have you got as leaders to save the world?'

'Many ideas by the way.'

'A leader can only lead if there is society. Society must be behind the leader who governs. A lame leader is like a blind man and cannot see into the issues of society.'

'Who is a lame man or lame leader?'

'You could be one.'

'What more have you got to say?' the senior leader said.

'Give people life. Stop putting people under your authority. Your authority is oppressive. You have suppressed people from talking their minds and you have failed to listen to their grievances,' Mr Batwala bleated.

'You are a poor man and you speak with confidence.'

'You have turned the nation and land into a complete workshop. Give people respite.'

'People must work.'

'Pay them.'

'No one deserves payment.'

'Give people freedom and liberty.'

'We shall arrest for seditions and treason.'

Mr Batwala left the palace and escaped to his village in Bukuku. The workers were busy on the farm. The prices of coffee were normal not much or a lot. Mr Batwala listened to the news that his wife had about the farm. Mr Batwala was filled with joy. The priest Father Motala had come to teach about the good news which he had. The priest wanted to convert him. Mr Batwala had known everything that there was to know about the good news. Mr Batwala went to inspect his farm. The farm was old and it was well known that all coffee trees should be pruned. Mr Batwala went ahead to prune the coffee trees. It was payday and workers lined up to be paid. The workers were happy and they all were filled with joy. There was no need to refuse to work on the farm. Mr Batwala paid them and he went to his office to listen to the latest news about the coffee prices. Mr Batwala sat in his office to read the *Financial Times* of London. He perused through the pages and read about how coffee was performing. People had no other commodity to rely on. There was news that other countries were dumping their coffee on the foreign market. The people knew that it was better to work on the farm than not to work. They knew that their fortunes would change. The change for the better. Mr Batwala was busy balancing the budget of the farm. He took out a balance sheet to calculate the overheads and to find out if he had broken even. He wrote down all that was happening on the farm. The facts were there to be seen. Mr Batwala called his workers to face the reality. He told them that coffee would make them rich but they had to bear with the little that the farm had to offer. Mr Batwala began to interview his workers; he wished to find out how they had coped. His wife had run the farm well. She was always on the farm. It was her only occupation and source of income. Mr Batwala listened to her version of events. She was happy that her husband had returned. She was relieved that her husband had peace of mind. She asked her husband to tell her about his forays into the world he had found. Mr Batwala told her of his journalism, his peace campaigns and his human rights fight for freedom on behalf of all people. His wife told him that he should take care of his ideas. She told him that she was faithful and committed to the marriage. Mr Batwala spoke to his children. Mr Batwala sat in his office and began to sip his whisky which he cherished. He was happy and invited the priest to talk about the state of the world. The priest insisted that the world needed God. Mr Batwala was in no way against God. 'God has his duties and man has his duties as well. Work is of the essence.' Mr Batwala was delighted to listen to the priest.

The priest told him that God would take away all his problems. He had to believe in God to help him. The priest said he was there for the good of the world. The world without God is a world of no meaning. The priest was trying to blame and accuse Mr Batwala of hypocrisy. 'You have to love God with all your heart and mind and soul.' Mr Batwala knew that it was his job to fight for his workers. His workers believed that if people didn't drink coffee then all their efforts would be in vain. Mr Batwala listened to the complaints of his workers. Yet Mr Batwala wanted to consult officials who set the price of coffee but they didn't barge, they told him that had to accept the order of things. Mr Batwala explained to them that they suffered many evils and their lives were detrimental to the prices of coffee being low. Mr Batwala asked them if he could set his own prices of coffee. But all that came to nothing. Mr Batwala wanted to coffee cartel to set the price of coffee. Mr Batwala spoke to his workers that they were powerless to force a price on the middlemen. How can a single village rely on one crop to survive? He was in a terrible vicious circle. He could extricate himself from all those that set the price of coffee. Mr Batwala knew that his prosperity would not last long. He was counting his days in vain. He felt as if he was working in vain. Was it worth for a man to give away and throw away his principles for the lowest price that man could come up with? Mr Batwala was not happy that he could have his way with the coffee prices. The prices of coffee were as bad as anything that man could imagine. The village relied on the farm of coffee. There was no other economic activity in the village. Each sector in the community relied on the farm existing. Without it all things would lose out. Mr Batwala was very angry with the powers that be that he could determine the price of coffee. Everything was being dictated upon him by other middlemen. Mr Batwala thought that they were cheating and the price did not reflect the circumstances of the ground. Mr Batwala left his office and returned to his house to rest. He was feeling energetic and healthy. He spoke to his wife and they exchanged experiences and all that they had seen in their lives. Mr Batwala went to his room and drew out plans of how to organise the farm. He had been through a lot. His life had gone through many phases and he was aware of that. He had made friends along the way but enemies were not far off. He knelt down and prayed in silence. He prayed for the wellbeing of the world. After that he went to eat and all his children ate. Some villagers who had no work on the farm came with bowls begging for food and they were offered food. The villagers knew exactly when Mr Batwala sat down to eat. Mr Batwala sat down across the window and time continued to be on his side.

Chapter Nine

Mr Batwala's Background

In the depth of Africa people were being rounded up as slaves to carry ivory, cotton, gold and cloth. There was a jihad, where they captured captives to force them into slavery. No one was of help and few were of help to free the slaves from their plight. No one defended the cause of the slaves. The slaves were made to carry slave traders lifting them on improvised carriages which they lifted up above their heads and shoulders. Religious converts were subjugated to follow the religion. They were told to give up their traditions. They were physically abused and beaten into submission. A child was born to whom his parents were sold into slavery leaving him merciless at the benefit to his strangers, who cared for the child who never knew his parents. The child was told of the disappearance of his parents into foreign lands where no one knew where they had been sold or if they were alive. The child raised himself up on the mercy of the people who lived in the village. Meanwhile, Indians slaves were busy building railway lines into the interior. The child was looked after by kind people and he was used to walk errands to faraway places. There was slaving trading taking place in the land, children, women and men were going and never knew who would save them. They were divided into opposite groups and they spoke difficult as they spoke different languages. They came from different places and different tribes which made them to use other mediums of communication. Mr Batwala was the child that lost his parents to slavery. He moved forward to unchain some slaves who felt that they need help and assistance.

'Why do you unchain us? What authority do you have? Just leave us alone.'

One chained slave asked Mr Batwala.

'I am sorry… I thought that I was freeing my parents. I want to go to a land where there are my parents. I lost my parents into slavery and want to follow them. I want to go into the world to search and find my parents. I was freeing you so that I can take your position. Whoever needs to leave the chains I will take over their position. Please help me to take over your place,' Mr Batwala said.

There was debate among the slaves about the situation of Mr Batwala. Mr Batwala was strong and he felt that he should leave his land and goes in search for his parents. He never knew where his parents where. He was going to inquire through all channels available to him. Mr Batwala felt the need to take a chance into being a slave rather than staying behind in the world without knowing his biological parents. He was going to take any chance he could take even if it meant that he was the only last slave to be traded he would take the chance into the world. Even if it meant going through fire or being dumped into the sea, he would swim to safety to find his parents. The cost to his life was not significant and no task was hard for him. Mr Batwala was convinced that he would continue to lead his life as long as he found his parents. Mr Batwala was determined to find his parents even world… which included his life. Mr Batwala knew that his life was not important without his parents. He would change the world if he met his parents. There was no problem in him turning into the slave of the world. He cherished being a slave. He was convinced to be a slave and he would work hard to be one. He liked being a slave as all things are made possible by God. With his life he made sure that he would accomplish all that is desired in his life. A complete fulfilment of his life. He would have achieved a lot for himself. He was content being a slave in a land that was not his own. He would endure all punishments forced on him. Even though he walked through fire he would still survive. He knew it was better to serve as a slave and be at hearts content and be stable in life. What is the point of your life falling apart if you weren't slave? He knew that he had to remain focused and forward looking into the present and hoping in a brighter future. Mr Batwala knew he was leading into a path that he could manage. He was confident that he was free in thought as a slave rather than having tormented and distorted thoughts. He would not blame anyone for his being a slave but he would serve. Even God serves the world by way of the weather. So to him it was difficult to serve. Mr Batwala was convinced that all would end up well. He didn't like taking chances of any kind. He was not gambling on the impossible but felt that he should turn into a slave of the world.

Meanwhile all slaves were chained and Mr Batwala had to convince them why he wanted to turn them into slaves. He chained the slaves.

'Okay, I have chained myself let us go and serve and let us go where we shall work and gain skills and after that we shall come back home to build it up. Fear no one, no fear of death or hard work. Let us serve the world and we shall gain independence to work for ourselves. Let us learn from others and we shall teach our young ones the way we like and offer them life to work,' Mr Batwala mentioned in an impassioned voice.

Mr Batwala chained himself besides other chained slaves who were going to be exported abroad. Mr Batwala led from the front without anxiousness but he was determined to go and find his loved ones. He asked others not to follow him in his path to find his loved ones. He did not resist being placed on the slave ship. He actually was forced to repair the ship as it could sink. He entered the ship and some laughed at him. He was led naked onto the decks. He was not offered any refreshments. Mr Batwala never knew where he was going and never knew if the destination would lead him to his parents. Even though he would not succeed he was determined to serve without any difficulty. Mr Batwala was aware of the punishment that lay ahead. He would work from dawn to dusk until all his life had perished. He loved to work and he never gave away his time to leisure. Mr Batwala knew that God would come to the rescue but the time and place he didn't know. Mr Batwala was lashed at by the slave traders and he was made to carry gold, ivory, porcelain, cloth, and spices which were cherished by the slave traders. The slave traders lashed at him but he did not give up hope but knew he was privileged to be in that position and situation which entailed going without water or food. Despite, all the pressure Mr Batwala gave his life one hundred percent to being a slave. He knew that one day he will have a great position in his life. The sea was against him but he would cross many seas without sinking into the abyss. He spoke endearingly about his parents that they had left him and as they had left him he was trailing them.

He knew a good son must look over his parents. He never joked about his parents' disappearance. He asked many people if they knew his parents. He wished to follow up on knowing where his parents had gone and what kind of parents they were in his time and if they loved him. He was told that his parents had been forced into slavery by some unknown power of the time. They told Mr Batwala that his parents were loving and would give a world a chance to desert their only son. They said they threw him into the river when they was about to be taken as slaves. The village saved him from drowning and he was placed under the custody of the village. He was more like an orphan as if his parents had died. Mr Batwala grew up calling each elder either father or mother. Mr Batwala led from the back as the caravan of slaves took two long days to reach the port. Mr Batwala lost weight but did not lose his will, stamina, energy, skill, focus and attention. He was completely composed and was jovial about all the prospects of going into another land to serve. If you serve you save the world. If you serve you maintain the peace of the world. Mr Batwala by the time they reached the port he was not exhausted but was healthy and strong. He was filled with humour. He was never going to abandon his life to perish but to live to see his parents. The sea was not frightening but it stood to separate and divorce him from his past. The sea stood to hide away what he had worked for and to make him a servant of the world. The sea never provided him with peace but only anxiety. The sea took away his identity, his existence of peace and created him a troubled tormented heart. The sea brought in him inner war and strife that he could just as bare and manage to handle. The sea created in him prejudices which he handled well. The sea divided and ruled over him and it developed in him strength to live a better. The sea did not provide good life to him but he had to make his life better than it was in the past. The sea drowned his ambitions and placed him into an oppressive existence which he battled over all over again. The sea failed to drown his ambition for him to be a man of his own make and kind. The sea forced him to take on new identities and to forge new lines of life that were compatible with his peace. The sea did not end his life and tradition. The sea can take away your identity but it cannot provide one with life to live. The sea is a temporary obstacle which is not with time and place. The sea tosses but cannot rule the world as it proclaims. Mr Batwala was not going to let the sea come between him and all that he lived for in peace. Mr Batwala left possessions which ended up in the hands of strangers. All that he worked for was despoiled and plundered or looted. Some things are irreplaceable and cannot be obtained easily. If you lose things they're very hard to replace. Mr Batwala left behind his cattle, sheep and goats to others. He had toiled for all his things and another had taken. Nothing belonged to him and he wasn't going to receive any help from anyone. Mr Batwala knew he would find peace in another land so long as he had found his parents. Looking for his parents was like finding an oasis in a desert. He was determined to find his parents. He was not going to give up so easily. His hope depended on where he would settle. He was not accustomed to being a slave. But he found inner peace of mind. Mr Batwala was not worried about his loss. He had to face two impeding situations of being without a father and mother and of being a slave as his parents. He chose to be a slave but not forced to being a slave. Yet as they reached the port they weighed the weak and the strong. They checked the slaves for any kind of diseases and illnesses which affected the price of the slaves. The slaves were lined up to enter the ship. Many slaves were from different tribes which made them speak in different languages which were not known by any of them. They failed to speak to anyone but remained disturbed that they could not speak to anyone. Mr Batwala left his duties which he was involved in and he was courageous enough to choose to be a slave of sorts. He was determined that he would work hard and not lose his sanity. He was not depressed in any way possible. He was fine and comfortable. His outlook on life was not diminished but was completely calm and composed to face reality. He argued against him being a slave. He never blamed anyone for him being a slave. He never complained that he was a slave. He never abused anyone for being a slave but knew that his destiny was in his hands. He never accused anyone for taking his rights and independence which he had before. He was settled and he was not in any way disgruntled by anyone. Mr Batwala was committed to face the world without fear. Death would not stop him from going along with his life. He presumed that life meant what one made of it. He had to make a choice in his life. He was not going to fail but to succeed. Leaving behind his homeland was not a problem issue but it was not a loss either. He left behind his home which he had known and he wasn't heartbroken but he was happy that he had left all his past life and was willing to face his new life in another land. With courage and determination. He did not mourn over his past life. He didn't lament over his past life but was celebrated over his life which was to come. Mr Batwala weathered the storm of being lashed at by the elements. He had gone through hailstorms but his determination was paramount. He was not deterred by him being called a slave. He was inspired by his willingness to look for his parents who he never knew where they had deposited in a faraway land. The ship sailed but broke down as it sailed to a foreign land. The slaves repaired the ship. Mr Batwala was in the lead to repair the ship. He fixed it and he was being lashed at while he repaired the ship. Mr Batwala told the slaves to learn the skills which were vital and would be useful in the future. They would use the skills learned to develop themselves. The ships; decks were made of wooden shafts and covered over by wooden planks and the slaves had not got enough space to seat or rest but were hanging by the stands. The slaves lived in conditions as those in a pigsty and they were congested conditions which was detrimental to their health. They fought over the space and the strongest slaves took over the running of the ship. The slaves were treated worse than pigs and they slave traders never inquired of the needs of the slaves. They were treated worse than Jewish slaves in Egypt. The slaves were canned and lashed at and ordered to work out tasks which they had no idea of working out. Mr Batwala involved himself in different tasks and he wanted to learn skills which he would later use in his future life of being a slave. The slaves were given water of the sea to drink. The slave trader captain of the ship ordered water to be poured and showered over the slaves. The water was got from the sea. The slave trader made sure that he leaves his slaves healthy and strong and he had to provide for them. He offered them food and drinks and made them eat raw food which was stocked. There were neither cooks to prepare the food for the slaves but raw food was available. The only food rations were for the soul preservation and attention for the captain. Some slaves wanted to jump ship but the task was unbearable. The slaves fought over the food rations they were being given. The slaves were treated as animals in the wild. They were like a game in the wild. There was no mentioning of their past but followed the journey to the very end. Mr Batwala was made to serve food to the slaves who were hungry and thirsty. Movement on the ship by slaves was difficult and they helped themselves on the ship. The ship stunk of urine and faeces which were decomposing. Mr Batwala spoke to the slaves to be hopeful. Mr Batwala meant well and he was patient to learn skills yet all other slaves never liked to learn skills. He knew this journey took him into unknown territories which he would find amazing. He was fearless and courageous. He would tower like a pillar of steel. Mr Batwala was relieved to find peace. He was being tested to the limit. He knew that whatever decision he made would determine the life he would lead in future. The choice of that decision was his alone for him to make.

The ship was being tossed up and down the sea. It restored the ship to calmness and stillness. Some material was offloaded and discarded overboard to lighten the load so as the ship not to sink. The slaves never knew the direction of the ship and never knew the destiny of the ship. They were blindfolded and unable to know where they came from and where they were going or where they were being led. The slaves were no allowed to see the sun. They lived in total darkness inside the ship. No day light found its way into the ship but only through cracks which indicated the time of the day. The safety and security of the ship was guarded by armed slave traders. They pointed their guns towards the slaves. The slave traders wanted to preserve the peace of the ship. Along the way the ship made stops to various places to deposit the slaves to potential buyers. The coasts were not welcoming but were a transfer of suffering from point to another. There were no celebrations to welcome the slaves. The coastlands were not home from home but were home to prison. There were liberty or freedom found on the coastlands. The slaves were gathered together to face a new renewed life of oppression. The coastlands depicted a land of toil, no peace but only sweat and suffering. The coastlands did not offer comfort but only allowed misery. The coastlands were not a good site to live. The coastlands were to deprive one of their rights and human dignity. The coastlands took away personal independence and freedom which the slaves had to be replaced by torture. There was no return to the old days that the slaves boasted of. The coastlands were a reminder to all those slaves that they were living in a land that was farther away from their own homeland. The coastlands robbed them of their identity. They were interpreters of all languages who spoke to the slaves. The slaves were given foreign names they were told remain with those names which wiped away all future association with their past. The names took away their identity. Mr Batwala insisted that he would not like to change his name in order for him to forget where he came from. He detested his new name and said there was no point for him to change his name. Mr Batwala was told that he would be killed if he didn't change his name. But that didn't frighten Mr Batwala at all. What is in a name? For identification purposes and shows where one comes from. The date of his birth was vital to his name. Many slaves were reminded of their past which they had not forgotten in the least. They remembered how Mohammadists came on ship looking for gold and ivory. They introduced sharia law on the land. They came with their ideology to convert people. They offered guns to rival tribes at war in return for slaves. They offered their Koran to converts and never traded Islamic converts but only traded non-Muslim. The converts became supporters of the Arabs who came converting and they remembered Christians who came with the bible to convert people. There came wars of religion. People fought over their religions and all took opposing sides to form one single belief on the rest. Mr Batwala felt that religion had replaced all tradition institutions on the back banner. That it had lowered their past as being awkward and uncivilised in the least. To Mr Batwala religion had diverted attention from the past to the present. To Mr Batwala religion had taken away long held traditional freedoms and liberty. Religion had divided the communities which once lived in peace as one single entity. Religion had brought new thinking into the traditional equation which was unbalanced and informal. There was no peace as it was before the dawning of religion. Religion to Mr Batwala had taken away all semblance of past peace. Religion had diverted attention from one being free and comfortable. People had hated their past and preferred their future. They denounced their past and never remembered their tradition or customs. They argued over their past and never liked any single bit that their lives had represented. People became used to their new lives which they felt were better than the past. They took on new roles and duties which they were not familiar with. Mr Batwala never changed his thinking. The people denounced their gods for a single God a God for all gods. They were convinced by that argument. They were made to believe in one single God which they went on to denounce their many gods. Mosques and churches were built on sites which were sacred to the local people. Mr Batwala was not converted to any single religion but remained believing in one single God. Mr Batwala was filled with courage to carry. The people remembered the way life was before they were taken in as slaves. Being a slave was worse than being a cow. Mr Batwala didn't step into any argument with all the people who had converted. There were India slaves who were made to build the railway to take goods to the coasts. All coasts are waiting for God and not only slaves or goods were a belief that Mr Batwala held up to. He knew that judgment was on the coasts. Most slaves had a coastline mentally whereby all their minds were always fixed on the coastline. The slaves were offered to new masters and the slaves were told to look up to their new masters. They were told to give up their old loyalties which they felt were quite important. The slaves forgot their past and indulged in their newfound freedom. Mr Batwala didn't forget his language that he had known before. The slave masters began renaming the slaves and telling them to abandon their old names. Mr Batwala categorically refused to change his name. He was told that he would be given extra work for him not changing his name. Mr Batwala was not scared of any work. He was put on trial and he was told he wouldn't see the light again.

'Why don't you accept the names we have given you? So that you can follow the flock,' the prosecutor asked.

'I was given this name and I don't like another. Will a name change the toil I have and what I have to suffer for.' Mr Batwala beamed and muttered along.

'No, but you must follow and conform instead of you being an outcast.'

'Is the name Mr Batwala against me? Where the genealogy of my name comes from I would like to follow.'

'How could you know that,' the prosecutor asked.

'You want us to get lost so that we cannot remember our past. So that we cannot remember our ancestors and where we come from. Isn't that the case?'

'Forget your ancestors and get on with work on hand.'

'I prefer my past and my present away. I cannot give away my past to my future.'

'I cannot examine you any further.'

Judge summoned the defence.

'It is good you did not change your name.'

'Yes,' Mr Batwala muttered.

'Do you intend to go back to your homeland? If so never take any one with you,' defence lawyer bleated in a loud voice.

'I know everyone for himself.'

'Never, never take anyone.'

'I shall return on my own.'

Judge; Case is dismissed.

Mr Batwala went ahead to lead the slaves in the field. The slaves had no shelter but shared their shelter outdoors, under trees and in bushes were they had constructed makeshift tents and shelters which could not resist the elements. They cowered under trees to fend off the elements. They were faced with cold weather and they had no way of hiding away. They faced the cold spell of weather without any thing shielding them and they didn't have any warm clothing with them. Other slaves played in the fields and didn't like to work for anything. Mr Batwala went ahead toiling in the field alone without any help from anyone. He called on the slaves but they didn't love work. He worked single handed without any assistance from other slaves. Mr Batwala convinced them on the virtues of work. But all other slaves refused to work in the fields. Mr Batwala was alone and he picked up grapes and made a winepress for the wine. No one came in to assist him in his task. Mr Batwala loved work and all other slaves were weak and not strong even though Mr Batwala was as weak as the rest of the slaves. Mr Batwala was like a donkey with a load which would make it collapse. Mr Batwala was adamant to live out his years working. Mr Batwala was out working for his own good. Every work offers itself relevant to obtaining skills. He worked from dawn to dusk. The slave masters never involved themselves in all the tasks. Mr Batwala informed the slaves that he was going to return to his homeland and they laughed at him. He told them he had enough skills to help his motherland. They all looked at him as if he was a dog. Mr Batwala failed to meet his parents as it was not conductive to trace his parents. He received news about them that they had died in the course to a foreign land. Mr Batwala knew that God would reunite him and his parents. Mr Batwala knew that he had a line back home which would put him in place with work. He had all the contacts and he had lost his life into slavery. He knew some people who would find work for him. Mr Batwala was taken back on a slave ship which had taken him from the land of Africa. He was happy and his spirits were restored by his desire to live in Africa. Mr Batwala began teaching people what he had learned abroad or while he was a slave. He built up the land which required skills. He was settled. He found time to set himself up in the land; he chose to set up a coffee farm. He was met by leaders who he spoke to in order to setup the farm. He was told that nothing like a coffee existed in the entire village. He held meetings between the leaders and people of the village. They all agreed that it was good that they would become rich. They were told that they would have any power to raise prices of coffee. They had to adhere to the coffee cartel.

Mr Batwala never forgot what he had been and where he came from. Mr Batwala went ahead to inform the slaves that they had to return back to their homeland. Mr Batwala worked in the vineyards and no one slave came to his assistance. He had to pick up four hundred baskets of grape vines. Mr Batwala made wine for slaves who were getting married. They all celebrated for having wine on the table. There was a revolt whereby slaves rioted over lack of shelter and food. Some wanted to remarry the slave masters' daughters but they were met with resistance from the masters. The masters treated the slaves as animals and not like decent human beings. The slaves went ahead to destroy the vineyards in order to bring attention to their cause. There cause was justified and they were backed up by all slaves' manpower. The days were hot and the sun filtered through the days and there were slaves dancing and singing in the hot sunshine. Birds whistled in the stillness of the day. People were involved in practicing arts of play. Mr Batwala didn't join in the activities that took place. There were taught to learn a new religion and told to forget their culture, but the slaves had to follow orders from the slave masters. Everything was forgotten and the slaves forgot their traditions and culture. There was a time of crying, sorrow and happiness in the lives of the slaves. The campaigned against all kinds of work and they resisted to work in the vineyards. To mention how free the slaves were is not exaggerate how much they suffered or toiled. It was believed to suggest that they were all happy and free. Man has to work however tough the situation. The slaves took up different tasks which they performed. Mr Batwala was called a fool and stupid man for taking over the work which he had performed to excellence. They spoke of him being aloof and not associating with the slaves. Mr Batwala was never in circles of slaves who never liked to work. The slaves mentioned that they were being treated as oxen. They said a good master must give a slave time to live as the master. Mr Batwala wished to speak to the slaves about the life they were leading and how to overcome it in simple ways. He wanted to free the slaves from all their problems which they found themselves in. he was determined to speak to them on matters that bothered them. He knew they wanted to be rescued but he never quite understand how to convince them on the virtues of being free. Time would tell if he succeeded or not.

'I am Mr Batwala and I would like to talk to you my fathers, mothers, sisters and brothers in this great slave endurance. I would like us to return back to our own places of origin. After we had learned skills and overcome all manner of toil. To take back skills we have learned here in the slave land. We must reconcile with all those we left behind. Do not mourn about those who treated badly in the first place. There is light in the tunnel to lead us to fresh pastures in our homeland. There is light in the tunnel.'

'We don't like to return back to homeland in Africa. If you feel like you want to return then that is your problem and not our,' spoke one slave.

'If I return to our homeland never mourn that no one spoke of a time with his people to return to Africa.'

'If you can't get on the slave ship please leave us alone as you found us,' said one slave woman.

'Why do slaves toil and earn nothing. Yet no one will know where all goods and services will come to them,' said Mr Batwala.

'Who are you to lead us out of all this toil and torture,' one slave man said.

'I have been in fields working and all of you refused to work on the farm of vineyards. I will set up a vineyard in my name in my own homeland in Africa. I am now free and independent.'

'We need no skills,' beamed one slave young slave.

'Never mourn because you have rejected your homeland and preferred to live in this slave land. You have rejected your past and your motherland.'

'If Africa is kind let it come and rescue us,' one man said he was an old slave.

'We must go and rescue Africa from all her problems. I am strong and I want to apply my skills to helping Africa,' said Mr Batwala.

'We have lost our brothers on the sea because Africa sold us to the world and never compensated us for all our work. We will not plead with Africa anymore,' said one slave young girl.

'Where has all that gold and ivory we carried out of Africa gone? Africa has lost manpower and resources. You are all Africa's man power and you are the envy of the world,' Mr Batwala stressed.

'I lost my brother on the sea and I never saw him again. There was going to be a shipwreck and they threw him overboard. Who will help me to find my brother?' one young man said.

'None of us shall ever return to the land of Africa.'

'You should all be free. I am Mr Batwala. Find peace in Africa. You will not lack anything.'

'Is Africa a land of milk and honey?' asked a young boy.

'You are not our mouth speak.'

'I want to ease your suffering. I want you to live in comfort and all that the world can provide. Blame no one for having failed.'

Mr Batwala boarded a ship and returned to Africa where he served the land.

Chapter Ten

Meanwhile, on the coffee farm, Mr Batwala went in his office to listen to the radio and he wanted to listen to the coffee prices. He was confident that he would employ his workers. He was bothered that he had failed to raise the price of coffee. He couldn't dictate the price of coffee. He was the sole agent of producing, supplying and delivering coffee wherever he exported it. Many people came to look at the coffee farm. Mr Batwala showed them around the farm. They inspected the farm and recorded the activities and how it was organised. Mr Batwala had been through a lot and he shared his experience with many a people. Mr Batwala wished to speak to people who set up the price of coffee. Mr Batwala wanted to build himself a mansion if the farm was doing well. But the prices of coffee were low. He couldn't go forward to building a house. He knew that he was in a fix as if he was in a trap which he couldn't free himself from. He was blamed in the village for disabling life in the village. He was blamed for bringing the village to its knees. People complained that he was arrogant and not being kind to the village. People complained that he was not considerate, failing to realise their plight. The people wanted Mr Batwala to intervene in all their lives to sort all their problems. They knew that coffee had brought blessings in their lives and village and it would sort out all their financial problems. They believed that all would be okay and fine. They knew they would avert any disaster which occurred in the village. The people of the village knew they had found hope and they were all optimistic in all their lives. The people of the village knew that they had found freedom and peace. The people knew that they would develop and find happiness. They worked hard on the farm yet they were not rewarded comfortably. They knew they had found green pastures in the land. The village people knew they would find no harm in the land. The people knew that they would find pleasure but all was not as it seemed. Some of them felt as if they were being treated as slaves… working for nothing. Mr Batwala assured the people that the land could not provide all resources apart from coffee and that there were no minerals which could be harnessed from the village. Coffee, he said, was the only crop which could be harnessed from the land. Mr Batwala informed and advised the village people that they had to use the best that the land could offer. He told them it was better to have something to do than being left idle. 'Idleness is a poor man's tool.' He told them that it was not good to be redundant without any hope but only to speculate over air. Mr Batwala was very happy and he went out while his workers were weeding, pruning, planting coffee, picking coffee and drying it in the sunshine. Mr Batwala called his workers to discuss how the farm should be run and improved. Mr Batwala wanted and wished that he could build an instant coffee factory so as to provide instant coffee to the world. He called on his workers to raise funds. People rejected that plan as being unworkable and not viable. He told them the farm had failed to breakeven. Mr Batwala said the farm was losing out and had not seen any profit. The lives of the people were in the hands of the coffee workers. Mr Batwala said they had to come up with drastic methods to improve on the farm. The farm could not provide for itself. Mr Batwala said he wished that they had a coffee factory which would ease some of the pain felt by the workers. Before coffee was planted Mr Batwala showed his workers how coffee would be planted and he showed them how it was harvested. They complained that there was too much work to be done. They were told that they should pay taxes to the exchequer. Mr Batwala demonstrated how they could farm the crop. Mr Batwala, from the beginning, showed his workers where to dry the coffee. He believed that the village people would follow him in his quest to become rich. Coffee as Mr Batwala found out was a poor mans' crop. Coffee couldn't make a man rich. Coffee was a slave crop. Mr Batwala knew that coffee would gain one freedom and that he was not free from poverty. Coffee was not like gold or oil. He knew that it required much physical work. A lot of work went into producing and it had a long gestation period. Mr Batwala knew that coffee had given him little freedom and independence. The government took over all the proceeds from the farm. Coffee was unreliable and no one knew how much would come out of it. Mr Batwala knew that he had to put in more work and effort if he could just make. He was never exhausted or tired by any means. Mr Batwala knew that coffee was a crop of patience for one had to wait for a long time for one to receive or realise ones dream. Mr Batwala felt as if he wanted to sink down his problems with a drink. He lumbered to his office to try and soak down his drink which he hadn't had for a long time. He called a young boy who he sent out for an errand to buy drinks for him. The boy returned and Mr Batwala tipped him. As he was drinking, Father Motala appeared. Father Motala was alone and he didn't come along with any priests from the friary. Mr Batwala was happy to receive Father Motala. The priest had a bag with him. He went on collecting alms from the workers. He said the Church needed funds. Those funds came from the farm. Father Motala felt as if he wanted money which he would put to his use (personal use) and he never told anything to anyone. Father Motala told his converts that the money was for building a temple of God. He wanted to use God in order to obtain alms. The priest blessed all those who had offered alms. He went forward to ask people to give generously and without fail. The priest went forward to offer prayers to all those that had given money. The priest knew how important the farm was in terms of offering money or alms. The priest was involved in a dubious business in the village. Yet he said it was sanctioned by the Church. The priest raised funds for himself. People were asking themselves where all the funds went. Did all end up in church and church duties? People were not impressed with the priest. They felt that he was not sincere with all the collected money. Father Motala was involved in setting up firms of all sorts as a front to raise funds for his personal use. The priest walked long distances to find or collect alms from people. The priest told people to fund his habits of heavy drinking though he didn't show it in any case. The priest left his friary by telling his fellow priests that he was going to find rest and he was taking a stroll around the village. They requested him for things but he declined to give away anything of substance. Father Motala desired to take away all the wealth from the farm. He needed more converts if he was to succeed. The priest sang songs on the way to make people ready for alms.

Father Motala built himself a shelter where he conducted his prayers. He gave people bibles which he sold at exorbitant prices. He made up or wrote prayers on sheets of paper and told his laity that they would bring good fortune. He read palms and wrote down what he called religious horoscopes which would bring good luck to all concerned. He preached in the shelter and many people believed that he was pious that he could not be disbelieved. Many people came to watch him set up prayers. People said Father Motala was good because he didn't isolate himself in prayer or hide away in the friary. Many people were not trusting of the Church that Father Motala came from. The priest prayed for all but he had to pray for himself as well. The priest was not alone in looking for funds.

Father Motala went to visit Mr Batwala in his office.

'Are you drinking?'

'Yes, I am.'

'Can you offer me a drink too?'

'Buy your own.'

'How much does it cost?'

'It costs the world.'

'Be serious.'

'What I mean is, it is the best in the world.'

'I am in need of the drink. The drink I hid in the nest was drunk by the bird. I don't know how a bird can drink.'

'It could have been a thirsty man.'

'I can't tell.'

'To tell you the truth any drink is more than what your church can afford.'

'I am rich.'

'Are you?'

'Please can you give alms to the Church? You have funds and I would like you to give something back to the world.'

'I can't afford it. The reason is that I have not enough to live on and I have worked for all that I have,' Mr Batwala said after sipping his drink.

'Honour your father and mother and give alms.'

'I will honour God but not man.'

'All honour of God is from God.'

'I will drink and God will bless me because I have been drinking.'

'You are a drunkard.'

'I drink because I want to drown my feelings and I am hiding away from reality.'

'Please give something to the Church.'

'Can you give me any reason why I should give to the Church.'

'You are not giving to the Church but you are donating to God.'

'Does God need me to give to the Church? Is he desperately in need for my money?'

'Do not insult God in such a manner.'

'I am being sincere.'

'I can't believe in any word you say.' Father Motala made a sign of the cross and demanded a drink.

'God doesn't live on human strength.'

'You never know.'

Mr Batwala sat down to listen to the coffee prices and he was busy being interrupted by the priest. He was feeling uncomfortable and wanted to send away the priest. Mr Batwala walked from his seat and walked around his office where he looked out of the window to observe how his workers were getting on with the job. He kept silent and he was sipping his drink. He had the feelings of resentment deep in his heart for the priest. He couldn't bribe away the priest from his office. Mr Batwala was now aware that all depended on him being courteous to the priest. He wanted to know why the priest came to him in his hour of need. There was deeper tension in his heart. Yet he didn't reveal it in any way. Mr Batwala was very aggressive in his approach and relation with the priest. He was uncertain about why the priest insisted on him giving alms. To Mr Batwala, would the alms end all problems in the world? Would they bring peace to this troubled world? Yet if alms were that important, would they bring peace to the world and sort out all problems faced by mankind. There was no point in Mr Batwala giving alms, for they can't solve all issues bedevilling mankind. Mr Batwala knew that alms were not important and that he could not in any way give any to anyone. Mr Batwala knew that alms were to rob one of his wealth to give to another. He stood in the middle of the office contemplating over giving alms. But he wasn't convinced that he would give any alms to anyone. Mr Batwala walked out of the office to inspect his workers and he found them collecting money for the priest. He told them to get back to work and to forget giving any alms to anyone. The priest followed on behind. He was appearing happy that he had got enough alms from the people of the farm. As they were collecting alms a deluge of rain appeared in their midst. The farm was flood and it went through the shutters in the office. The documents were washed away into the flood. The crops which had been collected were all washed away. The flood wiped away all that pertaining to the farm. The priest stood in the middle of the flood to offer prayers to all people who had lost things. Mr Batwala commanded that people save the files that were for the farm. As the flood occurred, there was a dangerous situation which arose. There came an earthquake.

People scampered for cover and they thought that their lives had come to an end. They thought that it was Judgment Day. They stood underneath the coffee groves praying and looking towards heaven to calm and stabilise the situation. They were terrified that they were going to die. Mr Batwala stood in definite mood to feel still. There were huts tumbling down and they were scared in all hope that things would be fine. Mr Batwala told Father Motala to speak to God to cease or his authority that he had imposed on the village. The priest could come up with any decision to end the quake. Many people were disgusted that life was upset by the quake. Tremors would be heard from a long distance. Mr Batwala rushed to save his books which contained major and important information about the farm. He was worried that what was set up with much effort was now destroyed in days and it took much effort to set up the farm. There was recourse for the loss. Mr Batwala was more concerned that his only occupation was now destroyed. Mr Batwala was annoyed that it was of the essence that the farm finds a way forward to run the farm. He was optimistic that the farm would be restored to its former glory and the pride of the world would shine again. No one was elected to face defeat in these natural disasters which occurred in the world of farming.

Mr Batwala was not heartbroken but was firm and adamant to fight on and never to give up by any means. Mr Batwala never complained of having lost his farm. He knew that he should be inspired by others who had nothing but had lost in the flood and earthquake. Mr Batwala was not going to give up on his work. The people came to watch how the farm was being put together. Mr Batwala was very happy that some of the farm belongings were intact. Mr Batwala spoke to Father Motala to tell God to forgive the world. To calm his hand against the farm. The priest while avoiding the flood stood in the flood to demand people for money. He told people to give all and he would pray that life returned back to its former splendour and it would be resilient to a point of heaven. The priest called on people to give alms and told them to repent. God he said was against the farm because people were evil and he would destroy it as he destroyed Sodom and Gomorrah. Mr Batwala went on to speak against the priest's practice and he said he would lodge a complaint to his friary.

The farm was saturated with water and the river along had burst its banks. Mr Batwala waded through the flood to save some of his items which were washed away in the flood. He was unsettled and disturbed by what he saw as a great destruction of sorts. He was not much bothered by the flood but by the loss of his essential material which he could not recover. Mr Batwala's children came to his rescue. They had to save their farm heirlooms which were precious. Mr Batwala commanded them to get over with the work on hand. He was always busy lifting up pieces of files and paper and he didn't have any standard way of preserving the files. All papers were strewn in various places and he regretted not being organised in the least. His focus was to save the files which could be saved. The flood left a pile of mud and dirt in the office that he had to employ people to clear up. Mr Batwala was less concerned about the damaged paper but concerned about his drink which had floated in the flood. Mr Batwala believed that the farm would come to life again without fail. Mr Batwala went to meet a district governor. He was a man of authority and much power in the land, a man of great influence. He felt that he should see him on how the land would lend him a hand and resources to improve on the prospects of reviving the farm. Mr Batwala was not disappointed in the least. He was told that the farm was great and the land would give him a hand. The same governor in the past felt that he should take over the farm. He felt like putting Mr Batwala behind bars if he refused him to take over the farm. But Mr Batwala fought back and he lodged a complaint to the national authorities who intervened whereby the governor stepped back from taking over the farm. Many people in Mr Batwala's district wanted to take over and to combine efforts but Mr Batwala was firm and stoic. He was fearless in his determination to lead the farm onto higher ground. Mr Batwala became a pariah amongst the people from afar lands. People spoke about him as being arrogant and as being proud beyond belief. Mr Batwala was not going to let go of his fortune, which was the farm. Everyone needs assistance was what Mr Batwala believed in most cases. Mr Batwala had worked day and night to set up the farm. He had convinced villagers of his intention and plan to set the farm yet they gave him the benefit of the doubt. He was not isolated in any way but was comfortable in the least.

Mr Batwala went on to contact his bankers to revive the farm. He gave them yields of coffee as security. He was faced with one problem of failing to estimate the yields. He was given a period to recover the costs from the farm. Mr Batwala was called a radical and revolutionist in the least by his distractor. But that did not hamper him in his duties. Mr Batwala returned home and he sat down to write a poem about all his travels in life.

A man may walk through darkness but there is light
He may not be able to see the light
There is a place and time to find the light
Where there is darkness, there is light
Can darkness hide away from light?

I looked and walked
There was darkness
I turned and there was light
I danced and there was darkness
I laughed and I saw light
I said:
Can one hide from light?
People waited patiently for the light
Is darkness the brother of light?

A fool will not know light and darkness; he will live.

Mr Batwala sat down in his house and finished his poem which had all the hallmarks of a man who had seen the world and what it had to offer. He was delighted with what he had achieved and was willing to share his experiences with all who liked. He had been the head of the coffee farm, a journalist, a peace activist, a man of the world. He had turned his hand at doing all kinds of things. He bore witness to injustices of the day and he campaigned vigorously to free all mankind wherever they were and he knew he wouldn't fail. Mr Batwala had been a slave in a faraway land and he didn't have parents but he grew up to lead from the front. He was confident the farm would find life after him. He was an old man. His hair showed all his age. He wasn't wrinkled in any way but desired to have rest. He walked majestically to his room and fell down in a slumber.

Chapter Eleven

There was a blind man in the village of Bukuku. Everyone in the village knew him and they spoke about him in various stories and conversations. They knew he was blind at birth. His parents had deserted him because he was blind. They left him in the hands of a foster parent who took care of him. The blind man had a precious jacket that everyone in the village liked and loved. People vied and contested to have the jacket, to literally take it from him and went in the village spreading news about how good the jacket was, yet people knew that it was the only one of its make. Everyone spoke kindly of the blind man. His jacket had good embroidery and it was sewn in America. The blind man had no money but only had the jacket. The jacket was his security and surety in case he was caught up in crime. The blind man went to beg for food as he was hungry and he was facing a complete garnishment. The blind didn't like to party away with his jacket. But revealed the jacket to his counterparts. The jacket was the only property that the blind man had in his life. Each and everyone looked at the blind man and they envied his jacket which all people spoke of with admiration. The village people wanted to exchange the jacket for something more precious. Not even gold was as great as the jacket. The village people, in reality, could not afford the jacket. They all looked at the jacket in respect and awe. They pleaded with blind man to part with his jacket. The blind man said, 'Could God give away heaven? If so, he could have replicas of the jacket.' But there was no good tailor in the village who could offer an excellent service to the villagers. The blind man was hungry and starved and he couldn't give away his jacket even if it meant that he would starve to death. He was firm and still that he would rather go without food than offer his jacket to the village. It was part of him to have a jacket, his other half as they say. The jacket was his friend, companion and comrade. He couldn't exchange his jacket for food. The jacket would comfort him in his plight. Everyone was hoping that they could buy the jacket saying that the blind man would give up because he was hungry and starving. The jacket had great fabric in make and it was of high quality cotton and silk. There was none in the village like the one the blind man had. It was believed that it was the only jacket of its make in the world. Many people took photographs of the jacket to find out if there was any jacket of the kind in the village. Many people queued out of the blind man's hut to take a look at the jacket. Everyone complained that their tailors were good for nothing in reality. Many village dwellers spoke of the great fortune that the blind man had with his jacket. Some spoke unkindly about the blind man and his jacket. They felt like taking away the jacket from the blind man. But the blind man knew all their plans and schemes and he staged resistance and opposition against all those who came towards him. The whole village gathered to come with plans to buy the jacket. The blind man said he would rather starve than hand over his jacket. People wanted to take away the jacket from the blind man as to take advantage of the blind man's situation. The blind was never left in the dark. He knew people were scheming and he knew that they were taking liberties over his blindness. The blind man was not offered help in the least. He was offered primary service because of the nature of his blindness. He was pardoned by the powers that be, he was insulted and many people were disgusted that he couldn't part with his jacket. The blind man was followed wherever he went and children followed his footsteps. They sang songs for him but he dismissed them. They thought that the blind man wanted to fight. The blind man had a loud voice which sent tremors in the entire village. His voice echoed in the forested village which left all birds to fly away in fear of fright. The birds crowed as they flew off. The blind man had no friends but only Mr Batwala was his genuine friend. Mr Batwala defended the cause of the blind man. He protected the blind man and he was convinced that the blind man had a confidant in Mr Batwala. Mr Batwala was like an aide decamp to the blind man and he offered him all that he was well versed in – matters of the social order that were not known by the village people. The blind man hardly gave away his jacket. His jacket was worn on good ceremonies and occasions which were staged by the village. The blind man knew that no one knew what being blind was… but he was proud of being blind and he could cope. The village wanted to put pressure on him because of the jacket. The jacket was displayed in public and the blind assumed that it was of significance to show the village that a blind man could have some things that those who have sight have none. The blind man could run and follow his path. The people were scared that if they took the jacket, they would fall in trouble. They were scared because the jacket was popular than any other jacket in the land. Many people were scared that their time had come to leave the blind man alone with his jacket. The jacket was passed on to many people. There were no restrictions to ask the blind man about the jacket. Many people were disgusted that the village hadn't any tailors.

Many people came to the village meeting including Mr Batwala. The blind man was called and asked where, when and who had given him the jacket. The blind man hoped that if he told them where he had got the jacket, they would all rally against him. The blind man had worked hard and prayed to God that his only wish was to have a jacket. Through all his sweat and pain in life he wanted to have a jacket of high quality. He searched the world for the jacket. He only wanted to have a jacket. All his work or through all his work he was working to have a jacket in his name. He couldn't care less. He believed that if he searched the world, he would come up with a jacket. As they say, "Search and you will find." The blind man searched the world for a jacket that no one would own. The blind man went travelling from one village to another village and from onc country to another country which led him to America. The blind man went on to give speeches to great congregations around the world. The blind man was not out of work. The blind never liked the way the world was organised for him in any case. The blind man looked for his parents but never got them as they never liked him. He was left covered all over and left for world to look after him. The blind man was given duties and he worked for himself in order to get a jacket. The jacket was the only material he liked and desired. He desired to have a jacket that no other person could have or own. He was believed that he worked so much so that he forgot that he was blind. The blind man knew exactly what the jacket was made of; it was made of various materials which came from the four corners of the world. The blind man felt with his hands the material and he was pleased with what he had got. The blind man went from country to country collecting all material for his jacket. His jacket was the envy of the world. No man could take away the jacket from the blind man. There are so many hands in the world that all must surely assist each other. The blind man assisted the tailor and the tailor assisted the blind man. Throughout his travels, the blind man remembered how he had got hold of the jacket. The jacket had stars which glittered in the sky just like the night stars. He was seen in the night when the stars on his jacket shone and everyone knew who he was; he was strong and capable of achieving anything in this world. The blind walked the breath of the world to try and find out if he could own the jacket. The jacket liked him and he liked the jacket. The jacket spoke well of him and he spoke well of the jacket. They were good counterparts. He was inseparable from the jacket. Wherever he went, his jacket went along with him. The jacket was like his pet.

The blind man claimed that his jacket was like all things owned by man but provided by God in one way or the other. The blind claimed it was a present from God. A gift for that matter. People said he was making it up. That he wanted to avoid his jacket being away from him. The blind was adamant that he chose to hide away his jacket. He knew that people would request him to give away the jacket but then he had to wear his jacket. He had no option at all. The blind man couldn't give away his jacket for nothing or for anything. The jacket was like Gods' handmade. To part from it would have meant to part from God. It all meant a world so good to the blind man. The blind man told a story of a blind man and a politician: there was a politician on the campaign trail and people gathered to listen to the politician give out his speech. The politician delivered his speech. He went to speak that he had a house and that he was married contrary to his opponent who didn't have anything to show for; he said he had learned in university about politics. He said he knew each and everyone in the village. He would deliver food to all people in the village, that none would go to bed hungry or starving in any way. The politician called the village to vote him and to reject his opponent. The politician said that votes will end all the suffering in the world. He said that all men would be equal and all would serve the world and never starve. The politician said with the vote hunger, starvation and famine would have its presence for the last time. He said he would deliver rain to end the drought which had devastated the land. All would be able to till the land. The politician asked people to denounce the politician who had no knowledge of what people needed. The politician declared he was a politician for all men, women and children. He knew all of them and he would help them out in all their problems. The politician called and summoned a blind in the audience in his constituency. The politician asked the blind man if he could tell the colour of his neighbours' shirt. The blind replied that he couldn't. The politician went on to declare that people had to have a vision and he had a vision which could tell the colour of the shirt. He said people needed him as he had a vision and would not fail to describe the colour of anyone man, woman or child. The blind man stood to ask the politician that he was taking advantage and liberties over his blindness. The blind asked the politician if he was righteous, would he sit at the right-hand side of God? The blind man went on to ask that there is none that is righteous among all politicians and that no vote would be given to the politicians and his opponent. The politician declared that he was not righteous to sit with God but was only speaking of the vision of man. The blind said is your vision more than Gods' vision that I should vote for you.

The politician abandoned his speech when he was being challenged. The blind man declared that all were the same and none had vision like Gods' vision. Therefore, do not take advantage over the blind as they have an inner vision which the earth cannot do without. A blind man's vision is better than no vision at all.

It came to be that everyone knew that the blind man was given his jacket from God. Not from God's hand but from the hand of man. We all have dreams but our dreams are never fulfilled. The blind man's dream was to have a jacket. He prayed in years or decades for his dream to come to fruition. Until it had been fulfilled, he wouldn't be content with all that he had to achieve in one class. The standard level to realise his dream was to work on it, until the end of the earth he believed that he was fortunate. He knew he was the torchbearer and that all people abandoned their dreams half way. The blind man wasn't for giving away anything. Forget Adam and Eve's coat of skins. His jacket was more than hiding away his nakedness but appearing to represent the loss of innocence just like Adam and Eve. It appeared that his jacket was well sought after by the people in the village. But they couldn't get hold of it in any case. Since childhood, the blind man had desired to own a jacket. He spoke to people about it. He asked people where to get the jacket and who could help him obtain it. He went from shop to shop asking people whether they had got a jacket they could sell to him. He checked catalogues to find out where and who could help him obtain the jacket. Some people thought of him being lost like a lost sheep. They knew he was out of his mind. He asked God that it was his only wish to own a jacket. Yet he toiled in the village. He started hunting for a jacket in various unimaginable places. He stood in the middle of the village and shouted out of all breath… demanding people to offer him the jacket and they all surrounded him and they abused him that he was wasting people's time to look for a simple thing as a jacket. But the blind man went on to declare that he was only trying his best. The people found out that the jacket the blind man was looking for was no ordinary or common jacket. It was more complicated and delicate a jacket and the village people realised that it was not the normal one. The blind man went to churches, mosques, monasteries, synagogues to find out if he could get his jacket from them. They all told him to go for counselling in the village as they could not afford to give him anything. He was sent away that if need be he should abandon the village and find some place to full fill his dream. The blind man went into village markets trying to find his jacket but the search was like trying to find a needle in a haystack.

The blind man went to flea markets and searched with his bare hands to find a complete jacket. But wasn't successful in any way. He walked the village from door-to-door trying to find out if he could get a jacket. He wiped dust from his shoes where he was chased away aggressively. The blind man didn't give away chance but continued to search. In some quarters he was chased away by hounds as if they were hunting foxes. But he didn't give his chance to the wind. He never cast his hopes to the wind in order to get a jacket. He was determined and courageous that he volunteered to help tailors try and make his jacket to his specifications but they couldn't. His dream was far-fetched but he knew he would achieve it in the end. He walked the globe to find out if he would find anyone to give him the jacket. He prayed to God to help him locate where to find a jacket. He was aggressive as one determined to find his fortune. Because of his poor state God heard his cry but didn't direct him to find his jacket. He had to search for the jacket himself. He cried in his prayer just like a child in the wilderness as if he was lost. He thought he couldn't find his jacket but it was somewhere between the woods. He had to be patient to find his jacket. He believed that he would come up with drastic plans to find his jacket. The blind man sent for emissaries to get him the jacket and to solicit for help to find a jacket. The blind man sent the emissaries on a mission of good will to the people of the earth. But the emissaries came back empty handed. But the blind man did not give up his hope to obtain a jacket. The blind man went to towns thinking that he would have luck but he was unfortunate. He never gave up on his dealings and on his trade mission. He went to fortune-tellers who read his palms but they all failed him. They told him that he was never to get the jacket. The blind man stood his ground and never gave up hope. The blind man went out to campaign to get good tailors in the village so that they could make him a jacket. But that was not a priority to many people. The blind man petitioned for help to have a jacket and sent out the petition to the politician. He called him to find tailors who would stitch the jacket. He was not scared or afraid to speak about his wishes. The blind man circumnavigated the globe to find his jacket but was not successful. Many friends of the blind man told him he would not succeed in obtaining the jacket. They knew he would fail to get the jacket. The blind man went to Mr Batwala to find out if he could get him a jacket. But Mr Batwala told the blind man that he was not going to help him as it was a field he wasn't well versed in anyway. But Mr Batwala gave the blind man an appendance which the blind man took with him on his trip to America. People knew that Mr Batwala was wasting his resources…

Mr Batwala who they said never could tell if the blind man would afford to get the jacket. Mr Batwala prayed to the Lord to help the blind man achieve his dream. Mr Batwala rebuked the village people and told them to seal their mouths with glue. Mr

Batwala was not happy with the people for having become negative. The blind man went to America to find out if he could obtain his jacket. He walked the length and breadth of America and found out that there was a Jew skilled as the only tailor in the whole of America capable of sewing the jacket to the specifications of the blind man. Mr Batwala offered the blind a great fortune, trinkets, jewellery, ornaments, rings, gold, diamonds and pearls of a precious nature to give to the Jew. It was on Sabbath that Jew could not take any money. But the blind man convinced him he was on a journey to find his parents who he hadn't seen or known for a long time since his birth. The Jew said he had to wait but he said that God would punish him for desecrating the Sabbath. He said that it was the celebration of Jews coming out of Egypt and all Jews had to respect the hand of God that had rescued them from, the hand of Pharaoh. When the days were over, the Jew said he couldn't work because it was a time when Jews under Joshua had entered Jericho. The Jew said he was busy celebrating when King Solomon's temple had been built. When the blind man met a Jewish man, he had other ceremonies to attend to. He said he was celebrating the day King David having fought Goliath in the greatest battle to save Jewish life from being extinct. When the blind man went to the Jewish shop, he learned that he had gone to visit his sick father. The Jew left a note to the blind man that all materials for the jacket could be obtained in Israel. Then the blind man heard from the Jew that he was celebrating a time when God appeared to Abraham and the Jew said he had to honour his roots and history which was like no other. Then the Jew went on to Israel for a pilgrimage to the holy land. While there he never consulted with the blind man. He was on a mission to visit all historical sites and went to the Wailing Wall and left his wishes there praying for the blind man and for the wellbeing of Israel. He posted a message on his door for the blind man that he hadn't forgotten about him that he was in his thoughts to deliver the goods. The Jew was strict with time and dates. He remembered all the things he did and he mostly privately associated himself with Jews. He isolated himself in Judaism and hardly ever came in close contact with non-Jews. He had no circle of friends but he always waved or passed his friends with a little chatter. The Jew had so many ties and it was Mr Batwala who recommended the blind man to the Jew who lived in Crown Heights. The Jew rarely left his circles in this tiny enclave. He lived among Jews though it was descript house he lived in. The blind man could leave all his payments in his pigeonhole and the Jew rarely opened his door to someone else. He was always locked in but only went out to buy essentials. The Jew was not at home but in the synagogue. The blind man went to the synagogue to visit the Jew but the Jew was angry that he was being followed by the blind man. The Jew said that he had to go and fight with his fellow Jews for the land that God had given them. A land flowing with mild and honey. He said he couldn't put his hand to sewing because there was a war brewing in the holy land. He said he had to postpone everything to go and fight against the Arabs, it was said by him that God put up a mark on the land for them. The blind man thought it would take years for anything to be done to his jacket. But he didn't give up hope. The blind man continued to pester the Jew and he knew that the Jew had made claims that he was the best yet he had nothing to show off. The Jew said the best day to do business was on a Sunday, because the world around him was quiet on Sundays. The blind man said that was fine with him as he believed that they had to agree with time. The Jew went on that they should meet on Sunday. When the blind man returned to see the Jew, he said he had an appointment with the chief rabbi and he could not fail to meet him at his behest. He told the blind man to wait in the cold in winter where he was freezing in the ice-cold weather. The blind man waited for two nights outdoors, whereby Jews passed him in the cold and they all knew what he wanted. The Jew had let out word to his friends that the blind man wanted a precious jacket, better than Joseph, from his father Jacob. The Jews thought that the blind man wanted or wished that he was like them in tradition. The Jews called him names as they passed in the cold. They swore why God had created a black blind man. The blind man was called to serve the Jews in the neighbourhood. The blind man was made to clean all Jewish homes before the return of the Jew. When the blind man had finished cleaning all homes, he returned to the Jewish tailor. The tailor was angry that he spoke to the blind man aggressively and said he had no time to waste on the jacket if he had assigned the blind man to wait for him. The Jewish flat had dim lights and when one went close, it made noise… like Jewish songs to indicate that there was a black man on the door. When a Jewish man came along, the sound changed. The Jew said he could not work because he was commemorating the holocaust. He said he had to stand for Israel. To mourn the blood of Israel. He could not work at least for five months. The jacket it seems could not be made or sewn in any way as far as the blind man was concerned. The blind man waited for the five months to pass and returned to the Jewish tailor, the Jew had left a note that he was attending a Jewish meeting and couldn't be bothered to serve the blind man. Then when the blind man returned to the Jewish tailor, he was told that he had received an order from Jews to sew clothes yet it turned out that they had placed in their order after him and he was told that his jacket would take another five years to mend. The Jew told him that if he wasn't circumcised, he would serve him. It was like the battle when King David insulted the uncircumcised Goliath. The Jew told the blind man that he should be circumcised by a Jewish man even though it was after the third day. The Jew felt that he was being put in a dangerous position. The blind man had no alternative but to go under the blade of circumcision. When he had healed, the Jew told him that he wouldn't serve him because he ate pork, rabbit, snails, camels and all forbidden food which was unclean. The Jew told him that whenever he passed cafes which served unclean food in the middle of their homes, he felt like turning the world into one entity which was Jewish. The Jew told the blind man if he wished he must read the Torah and give up on the bible to understand what the life of a Jew is; the Jew took out children to play and all the children had skullcaps. The Jewish tailor said he was occupied taking out children even though he didn't have children of his own. 'It is important,' he said, 'to teach our children their history.' Lest they forget. For them to remember how they suffered times gone by. He said he couldn't turn his hand to anything like sawing the jacket but had to teach their children the way the Torah commands. The Jew rarely spoke of God in terms of him having helped the Jews. The Jew knew he was chosen to serve Jews and not non-Jews. The Jew said he had to teach his children to be strict Jews and never to mix with non-Jews. The Jewish tailor took the children to Jewish schools which were rigorous and strict. The Jewish tailor said he couldn't sew the jacket because he had to sew the children's uniform and it was important that he completed the task otherwise he would be ostracised. The jacket had taken on turns, the Jewish tailor made sure he served his brothers first. When the blind man realised that the jacket was taking ages to be sewn, he asked the Jewish tailor if he could be allowed to take one of the children as his servants. The Jewish tailor felt that he was being insulted. The blind man said he would pay him a world of good. Then the blind man asked if he could take one of the Jewish virgins as a wife if he failed to make him a jacket. That seemed too much for the Jew. Why would the Jew bring shame to the Jewish blood? Then the Jew declined to serve the blind man. The Jew said, 'Why do you not send your jacket to be made in Africa… can Africans not make jackets?' He asked the blind man what sorts of things were done in Africa. The Jew said he thought they were hunters and gathers. The blind man was kept waiting outside the flat of the Jewish tailor. The tailor was celebrating his hundredth birthday. He was the last skilled tailor of his age. All Jews knew him and they knew what the tailor was up to. There was a party in the Jewish tailor's flat. Many Jews knew who the blind man was and he was reported in the Jewish chronicle by some kind of man from another planet. The Jews entered the party without speaking to the blind man. The blind man was left staring and gaping into the pigeonhole for some kind of answers why his jacket was being sewn. The blind man prayed in the cold for him to put on his precious jacket. The blind man was called in when the party was finished to clean the mess that the Jews had. The blind man peeped through the velvet curtains and blinds to see what was taking place in the tailor's flat. There were jumping, hopping and skipping. The Jewish tailor told them old Jewish stories and he called on all Jews to remain the same in one blood. The blind man was not invited and he was not offered any food by the Jews. The blind man was freezing in the cold. He made himself warm by erecting a fire which the Jews blew out for the blind man to freeze. The Jewish tailor told his brothers that the blind man wanted to rob the Jews of all their wealth. The old man said that Jews were helping the world as if the world needed help. The blind man was giving up on the Jewish tailor and when he demanded his payment to be refunded, he was sent away empty handed. The Jew said he had not made any signed agreement with him and he said he had given his lot to Israel and to all Jews.

He said if the blind man wanted, he should report the matter to the Jewish state. The Jew told the blind man that was the end of the matter and nothing could be done to rectify the situation.

Meanwhile, Mr Batwala heard of the plight of the blind man and he decided to take out from his clothes lot and he found a jacket made by the same Jewish tailor. It was discarded by the Jew and it was a donation from Jew. The jacket was like no other. Mr Batwala walked the streets of New York to find the blind man who he wanted to give the jacket. The blind man wanted to place the Jewish tailor in prison. Was the Jew entitled to all things in the earth? Why was he not accountable to his sweat? Mr Batwala met the blind man and he gave him the jacket. The blind man couldn't believe his luck. He danced in the street and he sang songs of joy.

He never lamented but remained happy. He thanked Mr Batwala for offering him the jacket; the jacket was priceless and no one could put any value over it. Mr Batwala and the blind man returned to Uganda and settled down. Mr Batwala had saved a soul of the motherland. The Jew and the blind man's position were irreconcilable and both could not come to an agreement, the blind was told to settle his case with the Jewish state. The Jew couldn't reimburse any monies taken as a result of trying to assist the blind man to obtain a jacket. The Jew claimed that the blind man had helped the Jewish state. The Jew went on to insist that the blind man should and must work for him as his own slave for an indefinite period. He said that he was a scribe and rejected all works made by non-Jews. The blind man tried to recover his funds that he had given to the Jew but with little success. He thought he had thrown away his money to the wind. Which wind had disappeared into the wider world? The Jew said to the blind man that whoever serves Jews is righteous and must be praised in all his work. The Jew requested that the blind man serve the Jewish state. The Jew gave the blind man tattered jackets that were discarded by all Jews. The Jew forgot all the teachings of Moses when they had come out of Egypt. Moses had told them to hold slaves for a short time and for them not to withhold anything from the slaves. When the blind man tried to explain the teachings of Moses to the Jew, he went into a temper which distracted his neighbours. The Jew went on to speak to the blind man that he had served the blind man by giving him his clothes.

The blind man debated, however, that how can a good jacket be replaced by old clothes which were torn to threads. The Jew rarely went into public places, only on important occasions. He never ventured into parks but remained locked up in his own flat. He looked out of the window at passing movements of people, looking into streets and he rarely strolled but kept to himself and never gave away any of his activities to anyone. He was secretive and introverted by all standards of means. Sometimes he took up time to teach the young of the teachings of the Torah. The Jew was seen buying food in kosher shops and speaking silently to friends who were Jewish and nothing more. The blind man meanwhile reminded the Jew that they were slaves in Egypt and pleaded with the Jew that he should release him from his bondage. The Jew prided himself on a generally held view that they had (Jews brought civilisation and enlightenment to the world), existed for a long time out living all former tribes like Philistines etc. and they had lived long in the world. The Jew made the blind man stand guard over his flat in case of any break in and he was made into a security guard to guard against armed robbery.

The blind man was told not to associate and involve himself in Jewish circles which life was assumed to be different from any other culture. He was told that the land of Israel belonged to the children of Abraham. He said Jews had suffered the world over and they should be respected by all men, women and children of the world. The blind man was told to guard all residences and premises of all Jews if the blind man was to realise his dream of obtaining a jacket. There appeared a flood which flooded the Jew's flat and the blind man was made to sweep out the floods. Everything was submerged in the process and the blind man was not paid for this task. There was not one or any item which was spread in the flood and the blind man took liberties by removing the furniture which he took to his home… without knowledge of the Jew. The blind man furnished his flat with the Jew's property and he claimed that he was allowed to take all property into his care. When information was received that the blind man had taken the property, he was told it amounted to stealing from the Jewish state. The punishment according to the Jewish law was detaining him as their slave. All Jews decided to strip the blind man of all his clothes and property. The blind man was sent to

Israel to act as cannon fodder. While in Israel, they assessed that the blind man had mental health problems and should be sent away as he suffered from Jerusalem syndrome.

Meanwhile, Mr Batwala found it hard to run the farm. He had to come up with a good honest plan to run the farm. He had to come up with drastic measures to continue running the farm. He tried to sell off the farm to friends but they all declined. They told him that it was not a viable project. They laughed at his plans. His friends insisted that he should give up and face privation like all of them. Mr Batwala became disturbed by how the farm became wasteful. No one liked working on the farm and people left it in ruins. What was once a coffee farm became a bush. The unpicked coffee was by now rotting on its branches. The coffee beans were ripening and falling off the branches involuntary. The beans which were rotten on the branches became heated in the sunshine becoming hard and a total waste of resources. Mr Batwala went on to inspect the farm and he was shocked to find that everything was rotting away. He couldn't save the farm single-handed but was out of all knowledge to save the farm. His friends told him to sell-off the farm or to auction that was the only way he could get rid of the farm. Mr Batwala's calculations did not add up and he was at a loss. All his life he was depending on to the success of the farm. All his life he was surrounded by the farm.

Mr Batwala went ahead to discuss selling off his coffee farm estate. He discussed with the villagers, church folk and high-ranking officials. He was determined as a lion to sell off the farm. Nothing would stop him from selling the farm. He would go to great lengths whereby he would put his life on the line. He never liked giving up as it would mean that he had failed in all his duties. He felt important to consult as many people as possible. He felt it important to talk all concerned. He wondered how one would buy the farm from him but that didn't bother him in the least. He knew all depended on the price of coffee. If the prices were low, no one felt like working and imposed on him a great difficulty which he couldn't extricate himself from; he was not bothered by all negative thinking from his friends. Mr Batwala was serious about selling the farm that he went on a campaign as a desperate politician to try and have people buy his farm. He felt like being a failure to run the farm. All his life he was dependent on the farm. He knew nothing else though he liked and preferred running the farm on his terms. He never liked any exterior interference which could hamper his life on the farm. Even when people gave him advice, he never looked into it but rejected the advice. He knew people were laying traps over him when they insisted that they were offering advice which Mr Batwala rejected outright. Mr Batwala felt like putting his house on the line if he had received a loan from his bankers. He wished to put the farm workers as collateral so as to receive some funds. But he met with little success. He wished to put the houses on sale and he wanted to sell off antiques which he had collected for his use and for his wife and two children. Whenever the point of selling off the farm and house occurred, Mr Batwala rarely consulted his wife. He left her in the dark to avoid embarrassment and the fear that she might leave and desert him if at all she had what he had to say about selling off the farm. He lived in fear of her because she was strict and never loved any nonsense. Before then she loved him and she was loyal and kind but as they got to know each other she became withdrawn and hot-tempered and she rarely came up with consoling statements which meant that there relationship was ruined by time and place. The more time went ahead, she became uncooperative and very insincere about the virtues of living as husband and wife. She was spoiled by time and place. She wanted grand things out of reach from Mr Batwala which soured their relationship. Therefore, Mr Batwala did not confide in her at all but kept his secrets as a surprise to her. She delved in looking for any things that Mr Batwala had hid from her but she didn't find anything. Mr Batwala placed posters along the village premises saying he was selling his farm and this caused uproar in all sectors of society. Mr Batwala set off on a journey to sell his farm. He came across a Governor in his provincial town and he asked if he could sell him the farm which categorically declined to buy. The Governor was in his official mansion where he was directing the people to be vigilant and conscious of laws which he was setting up. The Governor was seated on his office chair and he knew everything about the farm. He knew that Mr Batwala wished to sell the farm. He had asked his assistant to be briefed on the prospects of the farm. He never knew Mr Batwala in person but had heard of him. The Governor felt in his duty to find a way of taking away the farm from Mr Batwala. The Governor invited all clever heads to work out the way forward for the farm. The Governor was not in his mood and he had rested a little which caused him less concentration to the duties at hand. He walked to the kitchen where they were preparing food. He was hungry and he ordered for something to eat. He was offered a plate of rice and lamb which he devoured in less of a time. He finished and went back to his office; his office had pictures of the great and the good. Mr Batwala was among a group of people who wished to see the Governor. There was a crowd in the reception area and people were talking about several things. Some people were talking about the farm and never knew who Mr Batwala was, they spoke about other things, personal things which had come to their attention. They spoke in whispers. There was a queue that formed which spread outwards beyond the reception. Mr Batwala heard people speaking about the farm. He closed in order to hear what was being said about the farm. He was curious to hear what people thought had happened to the farm. He stood in silence in order to hear what was being said but there was exterior noise of builders hammering at the edges which drowned all speeches from the congregation which had waited for long to see the Governor. The Governor summoned one person after the other and Mr Batwala was at the back of the queue which moved at a snail's pace. The Governor decided to leave his mansion as he had other duties to attend to when Mr Batwala had got to him. The Governor insisted even though it was his turn to be seen he just didn't have the time. He said he was free in two years' time and never wanted to remain in his residence. Mr Batwala pleaded with the Governor to listen to what he had on his mind but the Governor said he had no time for him. The Governor, because Mr Batwala was persisting and insisting, decided that Mr Batwala's complaints should be recorded in the official duty diary and when he would look into the matter concerning Mr Batwala, he wouldn't tell in any case. Mr Batwala was disappointed that he had failed to give a good reason to see the Governor and this angered him. He walked away a disappointed man. As he was descending the walkway, he found people who were discussing the farm. He got involved into the conversation and he didn't identify himself as the owner of the farm. People were laughing that the farm had failed and they passed jokes. Mr Batwala went on to inquire if any of them could buy the farm. No one liked buying the farm. Mr Batwala stood silently unaware of what would happen next. Mr Batwala decided at last to go to the town auction parlours to find out if he could get any buyers who could buy the farm. Mr Batwala was asked if he could accept any price for the farm or if he could go for the lowest price possible. Mr Batwala failed in his attempt to convince potential buyers of the viability of the farm. Mr Batwala was told that no one liked the farm and as they were putting on the auction, they found out that there was no one who was interested in the farm. Mr Batwala went away heart-broken and he didn't cry or regret of failing but was determined to see that the farm got to its feel and its former glory. He had to come up with all the necessary provisions to make his life bearable and fit to exist. Mr Batwala wondered and got carried away that he had failed but that was not the end of the matter. Mr Batwala looked after; all his life was entangled in farm work and the life it had to represent. Mr Batwala contemplated destroying the farm but that meant that he was destroying himself along. He was prevented from doing so because he felt it vital that the farm was his life. The farm put the food on the table as they say. Yet Mr Batwala was the breadwinner in his family and had to take care not to ruin that existence. He was fond of working out plans in case the farm failed, those plans involved selling off his workers to other people who needed help from the farm and all it had to offer. As he travelled around the province, he met a man imposing and diminutive and he had worked on other coffee farms. The man told Mr Batwala that he was in loss making job and he said that all people had given up on coffee farms and that he should leave it to the world to run the farm. The man said that all farms were in the hands of all men. Anyone can take the coffee if they pleased or wished. The man said that Mr Batwala should leave his farm in the hands of the village to make of it as they wished.

The farm became dilapidated and ruined. It became a jungle and whenever Mr Batwala toured the farm, he was disappointed and he felt anxious of how to react to such destruction as far as the farm was concerned. He couldn't work single-handed and he needed labour.

Everything was lost to question and debate. Because of the state of the farm, Mr Batwala took on the battle. Mr Batwala wasted no time to heavy drinking and he wanted to sink away his pain and suffering to drown in drink, he drank from dawn to dusk. He spent all the money in the whole world that he had previously earned and he became withdrawn. He drank to sink away his sorrows and hopeless feelings which crept in his heart. He never liked facing the world and all that had befallen on him. He was bedevilled and this resulted in him spending much time drinking. He never informed his wife, Nalukuli, about why he had spent less time at home and why he had taken to the bottle. Nalukuli became concerned and she advised him against his drinking. His drinking interrupted all his former work. He was no longer that strong person that the village knew. He was no longer kind and never appeared in public at any time. Wherever he went, he took with him his bottle and never liked to face reality. He walked with his bottle drinking and speaking to himself. People mocked him that the farm had caused some worse state in his condition. People asked where Mr Batwala would end up. He was the talk of the village. Villagers laughed at him that he had failed to make his life as comfortable as possible. Mr Batwala, because drinking took much of his time, neglected all duties which he was supposed to attend to and he failed to manage the farm as frequently as he used to. The farm was in ruins. A lot of work had to go into revamping the whole farm. When Mr Batwala looked at the farm, he became depressed and agitated or disturbed. This caused him to drink and he sat in his ruined office drinking and looking at the farm. He told his wife that he was looking after the farm but he didn't disclose his drinking around the farm. He drank several bottles of liqueur and he always felt like staying on the farm drinking was a hopeless situation. Mr Batwala thought that the bottle would solve all his problems by drowning himself in heavy drinking yet it was causing him pain, poverty, and bankruptcy. Yet he never realised what the drink was doing to him. He insisted that drinking was like a remedy that helped to gain sense and stability. He formed his drinking to what a farm can do to a man. Mr Batwala thought that with his drinking all the problems he had would vanish and he would have any problem to think about. That all his problems would be discarded to the wind. The more his problems persisted, the more he drank. Mr Batwala was very bitter that whenever he had a problem, he would take to the bottle. He was corrupted by drink and he never gave away any of his drinks to other drunkards but drank all by himself. He lost friends who laughed at his pitiful state. Days passed when Mr Batwala was heavily drunk that he forgot to attend to his duties which kept on piling, creating a mountain of backlog. And this caused a lot of problems that he couldn't unravel all responsibilities. Nalukuli spoke against his drinking and told him point blank that he had been selfish not to think of the children. To Mr Batwala all that appeared minimal and never required his attention. Mr Batwala couldn't give anything to the world to stop his drinking… he would auction off his wife and children or sell the farm… yet he never knew where the next coin would come to afford his drinking. He spent a lot of money on a drink that he couldn't manage or afford. Mr Batwala made his house into a drinking parlour where no domestic work took shape. Mr Batwala sent out his children to buy him a drink. While waiting, the children came back without a drink and they had bought toys, sweets and soft drinks for themselves. Mr Batwala found out there was no drink in the entire village. Mr Batwala went to search the village for a drink. He dug a hole in the ground and deposited money in the tiny hole and went to find it but the dogs had taken it away. The children were sent again to find a drink for Mr Batwala but this time they couldn't return, Nalukuli demanded that Mr Batwala and she should look for the children. Mr Batwala went from house to house asking people if they had spotted his children. Some people said they had spotted them but couldn't say where they had gone. Looking for the children was like counting all the dust in the world. Some people said they had seen them boarding a bus. Nalukuli asked that he couldn't be relied on and Mr Batwala suggested that no country can do away without a coastline… that she had to rely on him as all countries rely on coasts.

Many people wanted to take over the farm. They went on to form rumours about Mr Batwala and many officials wanted to take over the farm. They made or defamed Mr Batwala calling him a thief and swindler of workers' pay. Some said that the origin of the farm should be established and they said they will find out that Mr Batwala had stolen the farm from some source.

As time passed, they knew that time was of the essence. Mr Batwala decided to give up his drink and the farm had not yet failed but what can man achieve in all his work on earth. The earth is a trial and Mr Batwala was tried by the world. The outcome of all his work was bent on luck… we all come, try and fail but life does not end in failure or success. The world is a place of toil in that nothing should be given in or taken away. Many people would find to blame others for their failure. Those villagers who had failed in life were blaming Mr Batwala. Investigations were set up to find the truth of the farm. It was found that the farm did indeed belong to Mr Batwala. Mr Batwala took out the "Certificate of Ownership" and many people were disappointed as they wanted to get hold of the farm. Mr Batwala was talked about in many circles in the village. He became a byword of suffering and of theft. When Mr Batwala heard the word come to him, he went ahead with his life and brushed aside all bad comments meant for him. He never became disappointed in any case. He was buoyed with confidence and determination to carry on drinking. His drinking heavily was caused by the misfortune he faced due to the failure of the farm. He couldn't initiate any drastic programme to revive the farm. Many people spoke of how Mr Batwala didn't complain that other people had caused him to drink spirits. He took his life in his hands and he didn't give up. He spent days and nights contemplating where he would buy spirits and how he could afford them in one way or other. Mr Batwala rarely saw his children and he was alone in the fields taking time out from all his responsibilities. He rarely appeared in public and he was the talk of the village. People went on to speak of him as a man who at one time took control of the village and they all laughed at his plans. They denounced the farm and never forgave Mr Batwala for starting up the farm. They were bewildered of Mr Batwala's condition which prompted them to suggest that Mr Batwala was a servant of the devil. They spoke of how they had suffered and how Mr Batwala was against the word of God, whereby he dismissed the priest Father Motala. People spoke of how God had come to punish Mr Batwala. They knew God would not forgive Mr Batwala for all his wrongs. Mr Batwala never cared about what was spoken about him in public. His future and destiny were in his hands and in his life. He faced the world. He was trying to run away from reality and a good reason to live. Drinking had ruined Mr Batwala's reputation and no one trusted him as before. He lost friends due to drinking. They felt that Mr Batwala was weak and not strong in any manner of the word. Mr Batwala was no way embarrassed by his drinking. Mr Batwala was the strength of the village. He came to symbolise stability and firmness of purpose. He was drunk but focused and he never lost his will to live. He lived his life to the full and he was full of life. He never succumbed to greed or corruption; his only weakness was drinking strong spirits. Mr Batwala welcomed all people to his home and he indulged them all in his drinking.

They said that Mr Batwala had become weak as he had forgotten all work on the farm. They wondered where the man Mr Batwala had gone or disappeared to but couldn't come up with any answers to why Mr Batwala had given up his will to work on the farm. Mr Batwala was ridiculed and insulted for his weakness and he faced other accusations over his behaviour and character. Mr Batwala called on the village to find its future and direction and not to dwell on him as the single most important issue in the whole world and he told them not to concern themselves with his wishes. Mr Batwala was determined to clear his family from his path. They all laughed at Mr Batwala's lacking will to live a dry life. Mr Batwala was not going to be given into the rumours that circulated in the village about his family.

Eventually, Mr Batwala had a desire to restore his farm to glory but had to take up work but became a useless drunkard.